The Christmas Card

A Novella By

Published by
Olivia Kimbrell Press™

Olivia Kimbrell Press ™

D1072894

Library Cataloging Data
Tru, Amanda (Amanda Tru) 1978-

  Christmas Card, The/Amanda Tru
    50 p. 20.32cm x 12.7cm (8in x 5in.)

Summary: A Christmas card meant to win the heart of a woman, changes the hearts of many.

    ISBN: 978-1-939603-92-0

1. Christmas 2. Holiday Romance 3. Contemporary Romance 4. male and female relationships 5. Christian Inspiration

[PS3568.AW475 M328 2012]
248.8'43 — dc211

The Christmas Card

A Novella By

Amanda Tru

Table of Contents

WHILE writing this book, two of my cousins I grew up with passed away. They were young, still full of life, and yet they were suddenly gone. While I know they are thoroughly enjoying their heavenly happy ending, I can't help but feel that their time here on earth is like an unfinished sentence. And the writer in me rebels at an unsatisfactory ending.

So I dedicate this book to those two men. Let any act of kindness, any inspirational message, anything good that results from this story be a memorial to the lives of Dustin Hammon and Brandon Soule.

May this book be at least a semblance of an earthly "ever after" for two lives that mattered.

LAST Christmas, another author mentioned something in passing that sparked an idea:

Do you know that, in this day and age, it is often cheaper to send an ebook to someone than a Christmas card?

That question, meant as a marketing idea, got me thinking. Wouldn't it be awesome if a book *was* a Christmas card? What if the book was told in such a way that it was entertaining, yet gave a clear, inspirational Christmas message—like typically found in a Christmas card?

And the idea of *The Christmas Card* was born. It is the story of a man who, wanting to prove his love to his wonderful philanthropist girlfriend, writes a Christmas card and sends it to everyone he knows. However, he in no way realizes what far-reaching influence it will have. What message could be so powerful to inspire gifts given selflessly, forgiveness offered through pain, and lives forever changed? And in the end, will it be enough to earn the love of the woman he desires?

I wanted to show the far reaching effects of a simple act of kindness and prove the blessing we each have in spreading the love of God. But, even more than that, I wanted to tell a beautiful story.

Unfortunately, when I got the idea for the book, it was too late for the current Christmas season. So instead, *The Christmas Card* was the first book I wrote in the new year. Though the inspirational romance / Hallmark Hall of Fame quality of it makes it different than anything else I have written, it still has a few of the trademark Amanda Tru twists!

Please enjoy this Christmas card, and be sure to read the Afterward that explains the project in more detail. As in the book, inspiring many people to share could have amazing, life changing results!

So here you go, World. Here is your Christmas card, from my family to yours. May it bring you enjoyment and inspire you to appreciate the meaning of the season!

Chapter 1

THE ringing of a phone broke the elegant hush of the five star restaurant.

At the sound, panic flashed across the beautiful face across the table.

Feeling the immediate glare of the Matre-d from across the room, Cole stifled a groan as his girlfriend struggled to halt the offending noise.

Cole gritted his teeth and fought the urge to grab the phone and answer the call with the heel of his shoe in the screen.

He should have known this would happen. If only he had made Sarah leave her stupid phone at home for once!

Juggling the phone into her field of vision, Sarah flashed Cole a look of anguished apology. "I have to take this," she whispered. Without waiting for a response, she pressed the button to accept the call.

As Sarah carried on a whispered conversation, Cole noted the increasing number of dirty looks they were getting from waiters and other patrons. Once upon a time, he might have been embarrassed. But this was not the first time Sarah had taken an inconvenient call in an awkward setting.

Granted, she had never interrupted a date in the most expensive restaurant in a two hundred mile radius, but still, previous experience had prepared him for this. What bothered him most was not the public embarrassment; it was the fact that he had made the reservation two months ago and had spent the time since then carefully planning for this night.

And now, she was on the phone as if they were munching fries at McDonald's.

Cole hadn't bothered listening to Sarah's end of the conversation, but by the look on her face as she pressed the button to end the call, he knew the verdict. After all, it would have been more unusual to make it through a date uninterrupted, than to have his cellular rival claim Sarah's attention.

He had been foolish to believe Sarah had understood how important tonight was to him.

"I'm sorry, Cole," Sarah breathed, her face stricken. "I have to go. It's an emergency."

"It always is," Cole grimaced, speaking under his breath.

"What?" Sarah asked, clearly startled and unsure that she had heard his words correctly.

"Seriously, Sarah. I've had these reservations for

months. Couldn't you have given me just two hours?"

"Cole, you know how important my job is," Sarah replied cautiously. "People depend on me."

"Let them depend on someone else for one night!" Cole gritted out. "You could have left the phone with a babysitter, for Pete's sake!"

Sarah looked shocked, and Cole couldn't ignore the hurt that filled her ocean-blue eyes. He hadn't ever spoken to her like this. He was usually so agreeable. From the first time he'd met Sarah, he'd known she was special, and he'd spent the last year trying to convince her that she belonged with him. But throughout the whole time, he'd been worried that one day, she'd wake up and realize that she was way out of Cole's league.

He hadn't wanted to risk losing her, so he'd put up with a lot. He'd stuffed all of his annoyances down deep, figuring they weren't worth mentioning. Just being with Sarah was worth minor issues that grated on his nerves.

But now, like a pot that had boiled too hot for too long, his anger finally seeped over the sides.

Trying to keep his anger-laced tone at a low volume, Cole seethed, "Just because the phone rings, doesn't mean *you* have to be the one to answer it."

Sarah paused, her eyes downcast and appearing to study the elegant white china and shiny silver utensils set against the scarlet backdrop of the tablecloth.

Suddenly, she looked up and pierced Cole with a direct, unflinching gaze. "Yes, I do. As long as it is in my power to do so, I have to be the one to answer it. Yes, I am the director of a charity, but my job is more than a job."

Sarah had obviously felt bad about needing to leave, but her tone and jerky movements said that Cole had pushed her too far. Now, her eyes blazed with determination and conviction that transformed her delicate features with an almost ethereal, spellbinding beauty.

Deliberately, she set her purple-encased phone on the table between them. "Cole, let me be clear. If that phone rings, I am going to be the one to answer it. It is what I am called to do. It is who I am. I thought you understood that about me."

Feeling as if he'd just fumbled the ball to the opposing team, Cole found himself on the defensive. "I know your job is important to you. Your dedication to it and your heart for helping others is one of the things I love about you. But tonight was important to me. I had been planning this special night. Do you have any idea how much I've saved to bring you here? And now you're leaving. Sometimes it seems like everyone and everything else takes priority over me."

Sarah's mouth stretched into a thin line, and Cole knew he'd angered her. Her movements were stiff and jerky as she flipped her long, blonde hair over her shoulder and bent over to gather her purse and coat. "Yes, Cole, I'm sorry to bruise your ego, but sometimes others are more important than you. For instance, when the temperature outside is in the single digits and a mom with five young children is left without power because her husband is in jail and she had no money to pay the bill, then yes, she is more important than you, your plans, and your fancy restaurant with over-priced food. And for me? I consider myself blessed to be the one who gets to break down doors at the electric company and do whatever is necessary at seven o'clock on a cold Saturday night in December. I *will* make sure that family is warm tonight."

Cole opened his mouth, but couldn't find any words. How could he respond to that? He felt like a heel. A family was in desperate need, and yet, in some respects, it seemed like he should still be entitled to some anger. Sarah was off to save the world, and he was pouting because she wouldn't stay to enjoy the caviar.

And yet he still couldn't help but feel like a disappointed child begging his mother to reverse her 'no.' Helpless to stop his own flow of words, he said, "But isn't there someone else who can help? Why can't you share the responsibility and let others take turns being the hero? Why does it always have to be you, and you alone, who answers the call and goes charging in to save others?"

"That's the problem, Cole. You think I do things for others. I don't do it for them at all." Sarah stood. "If you will excuse me, I have a priority to tend to. Feel free to enjoy your dinner."

With a casual wave of her hand that included the restaurant, the table, and Cole himself, Sarah continued, "If you truly thought that *this* was me—was something that I would enjoy—then you don't know me at all." She held up her phone. "*This* is me, and if you can't see that, then maybe we're both wasting our time and you're better off without me."

Before Cole could formulate any kind of reply, Sarah turned and walked out of the restaurant, passing the waiter who was bringing their gourmet dinners.

The red-vested waiter cast a hesitant look at Sarah's parting back. He placed the salmon in front of Cole and the balsamic sautéed chicken in front of Sarah's empty chair.

Cole propped his elbows on the table and supported his head in his hands, unable to hide his frustration.

"I think I'm going to need to take the dinners to go," he said, finally looking at the waiter directly, daring him to scoff at his request. Ordering take out might not be standard at a five star restaurant, but Cole was not in the mood for any snobbery. All he could think about was getting out of there.

Fortunately, the waiter quickly nodded, "Of course." Without question or judgement, the dinners were removed and taken back to package appropriately in their clear, plastic capsules.

Cole waited, staring at the empty chair in front of him. The rest of the restaurant's inhabitants had resumed their hushed interactions after the drama had left with Sarah. Though their conversation had been quiet, Cole was sure the tension and emotionally-charged body language had provided such a show that his name would be blacklisted. He would likely never be granted another reservation, even if he did want to Mulligan tonight and try for a redo, which he didn't.

Carefully, so as not to draw attention back to himself in any way, Cole reached into his pocket and pulled out the little black, velvet box that had been waiting so patiently. He held it under the table where draping red cloth concealed it from all eyes but his own. Almost tenderly he flipped up the lid. The diamond ring nestled in its black cushion winked up at him in a poignant reminder of what might have been.

Chapter Two

BY the time Cole stepped into his apartment, he was consumed with guilt. In his mind, he had not only lost the big game, he had lost it in the worst way imaginable. Instead of convincing Sarah Whitman of his love and asking her to be wife, he had presented evidence to the contrary and very likely broke up their relationship. It was as if, in the last seconds of the game, he had gotten the ball only to run it into the wrong end zone!

Cole tossed his keys on the counter, and flopped onto the couch, lacking the energy necessary to even deliver the to-go boxes of food to the refrigerator.

How did he screw things up so badly?

His anger and annoyance had left him as soon as the cool air hit his face when stepping out of the restaurant. And he knew he had been an idiot.

He loved Sarah, and he loved who she was. He'd viewed her phone as a rival that took her from him, but now he realized that she was right. Her phone was a symbol of her character. Her wholehearted devotion to serving others is part of what had attracted him to her in the first place.

Sarah was the director of a charity organization largely funded by their church. Cole had met her a year ago when volunteering at one of the charitable fund raisers. Since then, Cole felt he had followed her around like a puppy dog, helping her however he could.

Cole suspected that Sarah had initially only been interested in him for the skills that he could bring to her charitable projects. After all, he was a general contractor. But somewhere between building shelves, fixing holes in the walls, and roofing a needy family's house, Cole thought he had earned Sarah's love.

Now he wasn't so sure. Could his one faux pas completely end all feelings she may have had for him?

Though he would have liked to spend time with her when she wasn't on duty, it wasn't right of him to expect her to give up what she felt called to do. Doing so would require her to give up that which he loved about her.

Having reached the verdict of his own guilt, Cole's thoughts now turned to trying to figure out how he could fix things. If only there was some way to prove his love to her.

He needed to show her his love, but maybe even more than that, he needed to show her that he understood who she was. She needed to realize that, deep down, her priorities were his priorities.

Various ideas flitted through his head, but realistically, he had nothing. He had hoped Sarah would think the date tonight was romantic, and would understand that he valued her enough to take her to an expensive, exclusive place just to make her happy. That obviously hadn't worked.

He really was an idiot. Now that he thought about it, he knew that Sarah would not be at all impressed with that sort of thing. In fact, she had likely gone just to humor him. Chances were good that she would rather have gone to McDonald's and used the money he would have spent at Rinaldi's to help some poor children in Africa!

It all felt so helpless. It was like trying to propose to a nun.

Cole grumpily got up, picked up the two Styrofoam boxes, and trudged to the kitchen. Opening the fridge, he slid the boxes in, and then slammed the door with too much force. He stood there, breathing deeply and trying to calm himself down.

Please help me, Lord! I'v really messed things up with Sarah, and I don't know how to fix them. I thought we were supposed to be together—I still want to be her husband. I thought it would be easy. I would propose at a fancy restaurant, and she would say yes. That didn't work. I don't know how to show her that I love her and want to serve You as her partner in life.

He really did want to be Sarah's partner. He wanted her passion to be his. He wanted to help her help others.

As if someone had hit replay in his mind, Cole heard Sarah's words from tonight. "That's the problem, Cole. You think I do things for others. I don't do it for them at all."

At the time, he had simply brushed off her strange comment. Of course she did it for other people. But now he wondered what she'd meant.

Standing there in front of the refrigerator, staring blankly at the little blue light on the water dispenser, Cole was struck by a memory.

A few month's ago, he had gone to help out at the house of an older couple in the church, but mostly he'd gone to see Sarah. After greeting the elderly couple, he'd wandered the house to find her, finally locating her in the bathroom. She was on her hands and knees, cleaning the toilet with blue-gloved hands. Her hair was sticking out in every direction, and she looked a little nauseated and green, but when she'd looked up at him, she'd smiled. And to him, she had never looked more beautiful.

Even now, he couldn't quite understand how she could joyfully clean someone else's toilet like that. Many times, people didn't ask for Sarah's help; she just seemed to look for the most unpleasant task and got it done. No task was beneath her.

She helped so many people, but tonight she'd indicated that she didn't do any of it for them. Then why? What would make a young, smart, beautiful woman clean someone else's disgusting toilet of her own volition and be *happy* about it? What would make her *want* to leave a delicious, romantic dinner date with her boyfriend at an exclusive restaurant?

Truly, I say to you, as you did it to the least of these, my brother, you did it to me.

As if an electric shock coursed through his body, Cole jerked. The plastic cup slipped out of Cole's hand. He tried to grab it, but he missed, sending his hand knocking into the front of the refrigerator and the cup toppling to the floor. Water splashed across the linoleum and all over his pant leg.

Yet after the reflex reaction of trying to catch the cup, he stood, frozen and unflinching while the wetness seeped through to his leg.

He suddenly understood.

After several seconds on pause, trying to wrap his mind around his epiphany, he blinked and roused enough to bend down and pick up the cup. His eyes caught on a white rectangle that lay face down on the floor. He hurriedly pried it up, recognizing his sister's Christmas card. He must have knocked it off the fridge with his failed attempt at saving the cup. Thankfully, only the back of the card had gotten wet.

He rubbed it against his shirt, trying to dry off the moisture so it didn't affect the colors of the photograph on the front. Cole studied the faces of his sister's family—Jancy, her husband, and their two beautiful children—all smiling and smear-free. Below the picture was the simple words: *For unto us a Savior is born. Merry Christmas, Love, The Nolan Family.*

Cole liked that his sister still sent out Christmas cards. Nowadays, he didn't get many, especially if you didn't count his friends' Facebook Christmas pics that included the tagline, '*Here is our Christmas card*!'

There was something old-fashioned and meaningful about Christmas cards. The digital world was so fleeting; two minutes after the fact, the latest news was pushed down on your newsfeed. In a reality that existed largely in what everyone refers to as 'the cloud,'it was nice to have something more concrete. Those smiling faces and the simple greeting seemed more powerful somehow, more capable of creating an impression that lasted longer than the click of the 'like' button.

Slowly, an idea began to form. It wasn't as if a light bulb

turned on, but it was as if he was following a narrow, dark trail that gradually opened up to a clear road.

Setting the now empty cup on the counter, he abandoned the forgotten water puddling on the floor and, as if in a daze, walked to his desk in the compact living room. He turned on his computer and sat in his chair. As the machine booted up, he thought.

Once it was ready, he started typing. Fifteen minutes later, he sat back in his chair and reread what he'd written.

He hit the print button.

Snatching the paper from the printer as soon as it dropped, he held it in his hands, fully feeling the enormity of the moment. It was a wild, crazy idea. On the front and back of a piece of paper, his heart was written out for everyone to see. It could completely fail or make an absolute fool of Cole in front of everyone he knew.

But he had to try.

The copy place around the corner was still open. He could make copies, get envelopes, and start mailing or delivering them tonight.

Then he could find Sarah.

After shutting off the computer, he hurried to the hall closet and grabbed as many blankets as he could find. He had no doubt that Sarah would move mountains, if necessary, and have the Jacksons' electricity and heat turned back on tonight. But just in case it took a while, he would take blankets to help them ward off the chill.

Then he went back to the refrigerator. He stacked the takeout boxes on top of the blankets in his arms. If Sarah couldn't come to dinner with him, he would bring dinner to her. Of course, he thought he'd also stop at McDonald's and get food for the Jackson family. Even if they'd already eaten, Cole was sure the five kids wouldn't say 'no' to Happy Meals.

Crowning the tower of blankets and food he held in his arms was the paper he had printed off.

Though he would apologize and try to make things up to Sarah, he knew that piece of paper represented his only real shot at winning her back.

He had thoroughly analyzed the risks, the potential consequences, and the probable judgments of his plan. He knew what people might think.

And he decided she was worth it.

"YOU'VE got to be really close. How much do you have now?" Trevor held the glass jar up to the light and turned it around, as if he could unravel the crumpled bills and count their worth simply by looking.

Dillon took the jar from his friend and set it gently back on his dresser. "Almost enough," Dillon replied vaguely. For some reason, he didn't want Trevor to know exactly how much money he had. He'd worked really hard to earn enough for an Xbox. That jar was more than a wad of cash. It was a lot of hard work and determination to reach a goal that had seemed impossible.

"I can't believe your parents wouldn't even help you a little. Doesn't seem right," Trevor said, flopping on Dillon's bed and looking up at the posters stuck on the ceiling.

"I'm just glad they said I could have one."

"Yeah, but you had to earn and save every penny. How long has it been? A year?"

It hadn't quite been a year, but Dillon didn't feel the need to correct him. It had been a long time. Dillon had asked for an Xbox for his birthday and Christmas, but his one wish hadn't been granted. Finally, most likely because they were simply worn-down from his constant requests, his parents had said he could have one, but only if he earned the money and paid for it himself. They'd probably thought that he'd never stick with it long enough to actually make the Xbox a reality.

But he had. Dillon had done extra chores and taken every odd job he could, saving everything he earned in the jar. Dillon knew his parents still weren't thrilled with the idea of a gaming system; they were rather opposed to video games on principle. But he'd also seen the respect and pride in their eyes. He had achieved his goal, and that felt almost as good as it would feel when he purchased his Xbox. Almost, but not quite.

"So what games are you going to get first?" Trevor asked.

Now here was a subject Dillon was more comfortable discussing than the topic of his parents. After all, he'd been thinking and dreaming about this subject since well-before "Santa" hadn't granted his initial request.

"I'm thinking about—"

A knock sounded. Dillon turned to see his mom standing in the doorway, her hand poised on the open door in a courtesy knock.

"Sorry to interrupt, Dillon, but this is for you," Dillon's mom walked in and placed an envelope on the dresser beside the glass jar. "We got one, too. It's a Christmas card from Cole."

"Cole? Sarah's Cole?" Dillon asked.

"Yes, I wanted to be sure you got it before it got buried with the other mail." She turned around and walked back out of the room. Turning back in the doorway, she looked at Trevor. "There are snacks in the fridge, Trevor. We're having spaghetti for dinner. I assume you're staying?"

"Yes, Ma'am!" Trevor said enthusiastically.

Dillon picked up the envelope, barely hearing as Trevor mused, "I don't normally say this about moms, but yours is pretty cool, even if she didn't get you the Xbox."

Dillon opened the letter and quickly began reading. He felt Trevor come up behind him and begin reading over his shoulder.

He read it through quickly. When he was done, he paused, struggling to take it all in. Then he went back up to the top and reread it, this time slowly, trying to wrap his mind around Cole's idea.

Finally, he turned, handed the letter to Trevor, and laid on his bed, staring blankly up at the space posters on the ceiling.

"So your sister's boyfriend is going to propose," Trevor said finally, finishing and tossing the letter back on the dresser beside the envelope. "Is that a good thing or a bad thing in Dillon's world?"

"It's a good thing," Dillon responded without hesitation. "I like Cole. He's a great guy."

"But Sarah's not like... normal." Trevor's eyes widened at his own words. "I mean, she's not like other girls. She doesn't like to do things other girls do. She's kind of... different." Trevor sighed, clearly frustrated with his own communication skills. "What I'm trying to ask is if you really think she'll say yes."

Dillon's mouth quirked in a half smile as he looked at his flustered friend. He knew Trevor had been trying to come up with a nicer word for his sister than 'weird,' but the truth was, he was right, Sarah was kind of weird!

"I know what you're trying to say," Dillon assured. "Sarah is very focused. She isn't like others. I've heard mom warn Sarah not to be so heavenly-minded she is no earthly use. She's right. Sarah get's so wrapped-up in doing God's work, that she can forget about everything else down here on earth, even food and family activities. But I think Cole gets her and will take her anyway, even with her weirdness. If Cole manages to pull this off, then she'll say yes. It's perfect for her."

"So, are you going to do it?" Trevor asked, wiggling his eyebrows expectantly.

Dillon nodded thoughtfully. "I want to. I just need an idea."

"Hmm," Trevor murmured thoughtfully, perching on the side of the bed with his brow furrowed in thought.

Dillon wanted to do something special and meaningful—something that would really matter and help. He didn't want to do it for his sister, but as Cole had said, he wanted to give something of himself to the One who deserved it all. If that happened to help Cole win his sister, then that was an added bonus.

The problem was that he was just a teenager. He didn't feel like he had the resources to do something big. What could a teenage boy do that would make a difference for someone? Sure, he did little volunteer projects with his school and youth group, but that was ordinary stuff he'd do anyway. He wanted his gift to be different from the ordinary. After all, it should cost him something, right?

"There's that family at church," Dillon said slowly. "I think the dad is in jail and the mom is trying to take care of all of the kids by herself."

"I remember them!" Trevor brightened. "What are you thinking? Food? I bet your mom would give you a bunch of cans of food you could give them. That would be a good way to get rid of all the green beans."

"I don't think that's the point," Dillon said shaking his head. "I need to give something from me personally, something that costs me. It would totally be a cop out to donate my mom's stuff to them. But with Christmas coming, I was thinking maybe the kids could use some toys."

Trevor frowned, "Wait a minute. Wasn't your sister helping them? Won't she take care of all that through her charity?"

"I don't want her to," Dillon replied with sudden conviction. The more he thought about it, the more certain he was that this was what he needed to do. "I don't want to do something just because I'm assuming someone else will do it. Besides, I want to be the one to give them toys."

Trevor stood and slowly scanned Dillon's bedroom. "Well, you do have a bunch of old toys just laying around. Don't you also have a bunch of old toys in a box at the top of your closet?"

Dillon thought about it. He could give away his old toys. They did have sentimental value, and it would be hard to part with some of them, but that still didn't seem right. Those kids deserved something better than cast off toys. His gift needed to be his best.

But what could he give?

He stood to his feet and joined Trevor in looking around his room, searching for inspiration.

"Giving something that costs me nothing doesn't seem to be the point," he murmured to his friend.

Then his gaze landed on the glass jar sitting patiently on his dresser.

Chapter 4

"MOM, someone is at the door!" Benji yelled.

He pulled the curtain aside and peeked out the window. He thought he recognized the teenager standing on the steps. Wasn't he from the church? Benji's gaze caught on the huge stack of Christmas-wrapped packages in the teen's arms, and suddenly he didn't really care who the guy was!

Not bothering to wait for a response from his mom, Benji yanked open the door and looked up at a pair of brown eyes peering over the tower of colorfully wrapped boxes.

"Merry Christmas!" the visitor mumbled, his face turning red.

"Benji!"

His mom's scolding voice came from behind, and he heard her rush up.

"I'm sorry!" she said. "Benji sometimes struggles with patience. Can I help you?"

"I'm Dillon Whitman," the teen said, shuffling his feet nervously. "I go to the same church you do." He took a deep breath, and then spoke in a rush. "I hope you don't mind, but I brought some Christmas presents. I just thought maybe you wouldn't have many. So I thought I could pick a few things out, you know, things the kids would like. If you already have enough, that's okay, maybe I could… "

Dillon's rambling died out as Benji's mom started crying.

"Come in!" she said, trying to gain control as she urged Dillon inside. "I don't know what to say. It is so very thoughtful of you. I don't know that we can accept such gifts!"

Benji's eyes grew wide. He was almost drooling over the stack of presents Dillon was trying to stack neatly on the table. His mom better not give those presents back!

"Please do," Dillon said firmly. "It's something I prayed about and wanted to do. I know you've been having a difficult time lately. I wanted to help in some way. Please let me do this for you."

Benji's mom paused, biting her lip.

Benji held his breath.

Finally, she gave a swift nod, whispering brokenly, "Thank you."

At that instant, Benji's siblings poured in from where they'd been scrounging for snacks in the kitchen. All five of them crowded around the presents like the birds at the neighbor's feeder. With snow on the ground, those hungry little birds flocked to the feeder when the lady across the street refilled it. Just like the way Benji's brother's and sisters were now flocking to the presents like they were seeking the only seeds in snowy winter.

His mom immediately picked the gifts out of the chaos and held them up above everyone's heads. "You're all going to have to wait for Christmas!" she announced, moving to go hide the treasure in her room where the kids couldn't find it.

One of the boxes in the stack wavered and toppled to the floor. Benji swiped it up right before his younger brother, Sammy.

Looking at the tag, he saw it had his name on it. He looked at the neat, rectangular shape of the box. Then he shook it slightly, hearing the tinkling whisper of tiny pieces hitting the cardboard sides of the box.

He knew what it was. It was a brand new Lego set.

While his brothers and sisters whined to Mom to let them open the presents, Benji saw their gift giver move to slip out of the house unnoticed.

Benji took two steps toward him. "Excuse me," he said politely, getting the teen's attention. As he turned back, Benji tried to still the trembling of his lip. He wanted to say thank you, but his throat felt tight. This young man had come alone, and somehow Benji knew that meant giving the gifts had been his own project. There wasn't even a parent watching proudly in the background. He hadn't involved any "grown-ups," and had probably spent his own money on nice presents for a family he didn't even know.

"Why?" Benji asked finally. "You don't really know us. Why did you do this for us?"

A happy, little smile lifted the corners of Dillon's mouth,

"I'm glad I could help and do something nice for your family, but I didn't really do it for you."

Dillon reached into his coat pocket, pulled out a white envelope, and handed it to Benji.

"This will explain it," he said. "You can give it to your mom when you get a chance."

The white envelope made Benji even more curious. He looked back up at Dillon, wishing he'd just explain.

Dillon shrugged and smiled. "It's a Christmas card."

BENJI stood at the window looking out at the snow falling in the glow of the porch light.

He felt different tonight.

His dad had been in jail now for almost two years. As the oldest, Benji had tried his best to help his mom, but it had been hard. He didn't like for people to know that his dad was in jail. No one wants to have a bad guy for a dad. But more than feeling ashamed, he was angry. He was mad that his dad had even risked doing something that could take him away from their family.

Benji hadn't had anyone to really look up to for two years. It made him feel dull inside. He didn't want to be like his dad, and part of him was afraid he would follow in those footsteps, no matter what he did. But tonight, for the first time, he had someone to look up to. And he really thought that he could be different than his dad. He wanted to be the kind of person who did something nice for someone else, expecting nothing in return. He wanted to do something as wonderful for someone else as Dillon Whitman had done for him.

"Sweetheart, you need to go to bed," Benji's mom said quietly, coming up behind him. "Everyone else is already asleep."

"Mom, did you read the Christmas card?" Benji had given his mom the card from Dillon, but since she'd been busy, Benji didn't know if she had read it yet.

"Yes, I did," she answered seriously. "It is a beautiful card, and a wonderful thing Dillon did for us."

Benji nodded, then said firmly, "I want to do something like the Christmas card says too."

His mom smiled and wrapped her arms around him in a hug. "Benji, you do things all the time!" She placed a gentle kiss on the top of his head. "I don't know what I would do without you. You're the best big brother ever, and you're always helping me."

"That's different. I want to do something like Dillon did for us—something special for someone who really needs it."

Benji saw his mom's sad smile in the dim light and knew what she was thinking. There probably weren't very many people who needed something they could give. They themselves were the "needy-est" of anyone he knew.

But instead of saying what Benji thought, his mom pressed a kiss into his hair and said, "I love your heart Benji. You are right. There is always someone less fortunate than you, or someone who needs something that you can give. Why don't you think about it and come up with an idea. Maybe we can volunteer somewhere. We don't have money, but we do have time! Maybe something like that can be our gift. You get an idea, and I will help you do it."

Benji nodded seriously. "I'll think about it."

"Now hop in bed."

Benji obediently joined two of his siblings in the big bed. His mom said prayers with him, kissed his forehead, and said good night.

"Mom, are we going to church tomorrow?" Benji whispered before she left.

"I'm not sure," she replied uneasily. "It's snowing pretty good, and the van doesn't have snow tires. We'll have to see how bad it is in the morning."

Benji had been hoping to talk to his Sunday School teacher and maybe have her help him with some ideas about what he could do. But if they couldn't get to church, then he really was on his own.

Benji laid for a long time with his eyes closed, but his thoughts were swirling like the water going down the bathtub drain. Try as he might, he couldn't think of anyone to give a gift to. He was a ten-year-old kid. There weren't too many people lower than him on 'the totem pole,' as mom would say.

But maybe he shouldn't be thinking about people in terms of money. Mom always said that having family and people who loved you made someone richer than if he had all the money in the world. So maybe Benji should be trying to think of somebody who didn't have a somebody. Or maybe he could do something nice for someone who wasn't always nice. Wouldn't it be good to give something to someone who needed love, but didn't deserve it?

Benji's eyes flew open. Carefully, trying not to jostle his brothers, Benji slipped out of bed and padded back to the window. He couldn't see much beyond the shower of snow falling in the beam of the porch light. But even though he couldn't see it, he knew what was across the street.

The Christmas Card
38

"WHAT are those kids doing now?" Iris Lankford mumbled as she looked out her front window.

Here she thought that all the snow would keep the little troublemakers inside today for a change. But here they were, already out first thing on a Sunday morning, and in *her* yard!

Those kids shouldn't even be outside on a Sunday. If their mother had any kind of character, she would have those kids in church. Iris wished she was in church herself. Sunday was the absolute worst day for snow. She didn't like to drive on bad roads, and Rob, the man she usually paid to shovel her sidewalks, refused to work on Sundays. She'd have to figure out something. Maybe she could offer Rob double to come out and do it.

According to the bylaws of the subdivision, owners were required to keep their sidewalks free from ice and snow. Her pride would not allow for even a small deviation from the rules. After all, when you lived on Mockingbird Lane, it was important to keep up appearances. Some things, like sidewalks piled with snow, or ragged kids running all over, just didn't belong.

She watched as the four children traipsed up and down the sidewalk in front of her house. At least the toddler wasn't around to run all over the place. Thankfully, the mom likely had enough sense to keep that youngest one inside. However, that still didn't give a good excuse for why she was allowing her other four to trespass on her property.

What were they actually doing? Iris squinted her eyes, but the snow was so bright and piled up just right to prevent her from seeing the details of what was going on. Looking at the big pile of snow the children seemed to be amassing, she suddenly startled.

Were they trying to build a *snowman* in her yard?

Iris's lips pursed into a thin line. She really needed to talk to the homeowners association. This situation with that woman and her passel of kids was getting out of hand. It was bad for the neighborhood. She knew the family was in need; she'd even heard that the dad was in prison, as scandalous as that sounded. But there were places for the needy. Iris knew; after all, she gave generously to numerous charities. But her upscale neighborhood was not one of them.

Iris really did believe people had the right to do what they wanted with their property, within reason of course. But a line had to be drawn when something affected everyone on the street. And having those kind of people around had a definite effect. Her own house probably wouldn't be worth nearly so much if it was known that a criminal's family was staying across the street!

It just wasn't right. She would have bit her tongue about the Nielsons letting the family stay in their guest house, but her attitude changed entirely when the Nielsons took off for Europe and left the riffraff here! If homeowners were going to allow unsavory persons to stay in their homes or guest houses, then they needed to be the ones responsible, which meant not taking off to Europe!

It wasn't as if Iris hadn't made an effort to handle things herself. She had repeatedly confronted the children about their behavior, instructing them to stay in their own yard, yet they still ran around the neighborhood like vandals, holding races down the sidewalks and repeatedly, 'accidentally' hitting balls into other people's yards.

Mockingbird Lane was supposed to be a nice, quiet neighborhood, but it hadn't been since *they* had moved in. Iris had even threatened to call the police on them when they were being so loud she could hear them as she stood at her window inside. Then she'd had to go over and personally talk to that irresponsible mother when she'd found litter in her yard that could have only come from them. That oldest boy had denied that the trash was theirs, but Iris knew better. Those five kids were the only free range undesirables in the neighborhood.

Now it looked as if she was going to have to get all of her cold weather gear on, just to go out and shoo those little brats to their side of the street. She didn't even understand what they were doing here. And on a Sunday no less! She'd told them repeatedly never to set foot on her property, yet they were moving to and fro on the sidewalk in front of her house, just as bold as day.

If Jasper was alive, Iris would have made him go out and

take care of the situation. The corners of Iris's stern scowl turned up slightly in spite of herself. She well knew that her late husband would have been more likely to go join the children than march out and scold them. But Jasper hadn't been the most sensible of men.

But when they started wandering onto her driveway, Iris knew she had to do something, and do it herself. It wasn't just that they were trespassing on her property, they were ruining her day!

Since she couldn't go to church, she'd been looking forward to sitting with a cup of tea and watching the birds out the window at the bird feeder. But, no matter how hungry they were, the little birds wouldn't come near the feeder with those kids loitering around.

Determined to not tolerate one more minute of their impudence, Iris put her warm boots over her carefully pressed slacks, and her warmest down coat over her angora sweater. She zipped the coat up to the top and then fastened the buttons. Not wanting any chance of moisture slipping in to ruin her clothes, she wrapped her scarf securely around her neck and carefully poised a hat atop her styled and sprayed hair.

She then marched out her front door and stopped short at the sight of the four little faces looking up at her from *her* driveway. She took a deep breath, ready to let loose a lecture that would set the little hoodlums on the straight and narrow.

Then she saw their wet, sneakered feet standing on the sidewalk. Not on snow, but on cleared concrete. She saw the shovels in their hands. The oldest one had a regular snow shovel, but the younger three had little, brightly-colored, plastic, cheap ones that were more toys than actual functioning tools. She looked down at her own snow boots, seeing that they too were not standing in the snow, but on the concrete.

Then she looked back at their upturned faces, reading fear in their eyes.

Iris swallowed with difficulty. "You shoveled my sidewalks?" she asked, her voice airy as it tried to get around the lump still lodged in her throat.

"Yes, ma'am," the oldest boy said firmly.

"Why?" Iris asked, still feeling numb with shock.

"Because they needed shoveling," the boy said. "You needed help, and we wanted to do something nice for you."

Iris nodded, but her mind couldn't form any more coherent thoughts other than a quiet, "Thank you."

The boy nodded. "We're almost done with the driveway."

Without another word, the boy once again started pushing the shovel through the snow, turning it with difficulty, and dumping a load of the white stuff to the side. The rest of his siblings quickly followed suit, imitating their older brother's motions with their toy props.

It was hard work. Iris watched in stunned silence as the boy put all his weight into pushing the shovel. A few times, it seemed as if the weight and effort with the shovel, would lift the boy off the ground like a teeter totter.

Iris stared, but she couldn't help it. All she could think about was how awful she'd treated these little kids, and yet here they were, doing something to help her.

Finally, the boy looked up and smiled, "All done! Have a good evening, Mrs. Lankford." He then picked the shovel up and started walking toward his own house, the small cottage nestled behind the house straight across Mockingbird Lane.

"Excuse me!" Iris said, calling out to the boy before he crossed the street. "Was it your mother's idea for you to come and shovel my sidewalks?"

"No," the boy said, looking unsure, as if he might be in trouble.

Iris spoke quickly. "It was a very thoughtful thing to do. Thank you." Iris felt a surge of joy at the sight of the boy's smile of relief. "But I still don't understand why you did it for me."

The boy reached into his pocket, rummaging around until he found a folded, slightly crumpled envelope. He walked to Iris and held it out to her. "I didn't really do it for you."

Iris automatically took the envelope. "What is this?" Iris said, gingerly holding the gift as if she wasn't quite sure what foreign substances it had contacted in the boy's pocket.

With a parting grin, the boy turned back toward his house. "It's a Christmas card," he called cheerfully. "Merry Christmas, Mrs. Lankford!"

IRIS held the paper in her trembling hand and read it for what must have been the tenth time. She felt the warm tears stream down her face, but she paid them no heed. Understanding the extent of what that boy had done was humbling and inspiring.

Iris set the paper gently on the table and mindlessly wandered through her house, touching her treasures and knickknacks here and there without her mind actually being engaged in her actions.

Jasper had left Iris well-off financially, and Iris prided herself on the fact that she regularly donated to various charities. But Iris's work had primarily been in paying someone else to do the work or providing the means to get it done. She had never done something personal that had cost her as it had that boy. He had worked hard. She had seen the perspiration on his face and knew how difficult shoveling that much snow must have been, especially for a boy. Even Rob, with all his girth, was out of breath after shoveling the sidewalks and driveway.

After seeing what the boy had done and reading the Christmas card, Iris suddenly felt small. Iris didn't think of herself as conceited, but she was used to feeling like she was of a higher class than most of those around her. She was smarter, more educated, wealthier, and had generally higher principles than most others. Now, for the first time, Iris felt as if she didn't quite measure up. On the outside, maybe she was better than other people, but on the inside, for what counted, that little boy was in a higher class than she was.

Going to church and doing the right thing on paper wasn't really what mattered. She needed to do something more meaningful than write a check. If she was to give a gift, especially one of this importance, then it had to cost her something. It had to be a sacrifice.

Her mind started turning, trying to think of how she could reach outside of her comfort zone to give a personal gift that would impact the world of someone in need.

Desperate for ideas, she went to her office, pulled out the drawers of her file cabinet, and started sifting through her records of charitable giving. Most of the charities weren't even in the area. Some were even overseas, but maybe she could call one of them and find out if there was a special need.

She grimaced. That still wouldn't really fulfill her heart's desire. She would still be writing a check and having someone meet the need. She needed to do something local that would require a sacrifice of her time and energy.

Her eyes caught on the words "Volunteers Needed." Iris pulled out the flier she had filed with her charitable giving receipts, read the paper, and then paused, focusing on the address of the facility. Her heart leapt in both excitement and stark fear. Then she set her jaw, nodded, and pushed the file cabinet closed.

Iris Lankford had found her sacrifice.

Chapter Six

HENRY noticed her the instant she stepped through the door. He wasn't an overly observant man; he usually just ate his meal and left, minding his own business. But she was kind of hard to miss.

She wore a bright white shirt with a blue jacket and matching blue skirt, while her feet boasted heels in the exact same shade of blue.

Henry had never seen anyone like her step into a soup kitchen before.

Even from this distance, it was clear she didn't belong. And what was worse was that she knew it. Her mouth was a thin line, her jaw was tensed, and every muscle in her body looked stiff.

A memory whispered through Henry's mind. He and several other soldiers were combing over a battlefield, looking for survivors, the day after the fighting had moved on. The ground was blackened, with more debris than vegetation littering the landscape. Smoke still curled out of the ground in places. In the midst of the devastation, Henry caught sight of a little blue flower, poking its dainty head up out of the blackened earth. He didn't know what it was called, but it looked like a type of violet. What was most striking was that it was completely untouched, as if it belonged in a different dimension than the world around it.

As then, Henry now felt a similar sense of reverence and awe as he looked at the woman in blue. She was a flower in the battlefield of a soup kitchen for the homeless.

Mentally dubbing her the 'Blue Violet,' Henry watched as she jerkily scanned the large room, and then headed directly to the kitchen, her heels tapping smartly on the dull linoleum.

Henry saw her speaking to one of the workers, but lost sight of her when she went into the kitchen itself.

A few minutes later, the minister said a prayer over the food, and everyone lined up in a long queue for the food. As usual, Henry stayed where he was, waiting until everyone else was through the line. Though he was hungry, it wasn't worth standing when he could be comfortably sitting and get his food after the busyness had subsided.

Henry watched the homeless lined up for the free meal and thought what a sorry lot they all were. The group was mostly men, scruffy and unshaven with dirty clothes, looking very much like the homeless stereotype. There were a few standouts in the group—a few women and one or two families with children. But usually women and families who'd fallen on hard times ended up in one of the other homeless shelters that better fit their needs. This place catered more to the lone men, and after having taken meals here for a couple months, Henry could recognize the regulars.

Finally, the last of the diners were being served through the line, and Henry stood and lumbered over. He nodded appreciatively as each worker in the assembly line contributed food to his tray. Today's fare included baked chicken, mashed potatoes, and green beans.

Last in line was the woman in blue, Henry's Blue Violet, serving dessert. She dutifully placed a piece of carrot cake on his tray.

But instead of moving on, Henry paused and looked at her.

He reached up with one hand, feeling the itchy stubble of his beard, and he knew how he must look to her. He made it a point to get regular showers at various homeless shelters, but he was wearing all the clothes he owned in layers, and every single piece was threadbare.

Nevertheless, Henry lifted his head and met the Blue Violet's eyes. "Please don't take this the wrong way, ma'am, but what is a gal like you doing in a place like this?"

A soft blush crept up the Blue Violet's cheeks, but she didn't seem upset. In fact, the corners of her mouth curled up slightly, as if in amusement. "I'm a volunteer," she responded quietly.

Henry nodded. "I see new volunteers around here every once in a while, but I usually only see the new faces once. I don't know if they are just curious about what a soup kitchen really is like, or if they volunteer here once and then find a better gig."

The Blue Violet lifted her head up tall, looking

determined. "I'll be volunteering one day a week for the foreseeable future. If you're here this time next week, then you'll see my face again."

Henry grinned. "Well, then, that is a sight I will be looking forward to."

Seemingly flustered, the spatula in the Blue Violet's hand slipped from her grip. She made a grab for it, but she missed. It hit her arm and then knocked into the front of her skirt. The spatula clattered to the floor, leaving a trail of white cream cheese frosting on the arm and the skirt of her tailored suit.

The Blue Violet grabbed a napkin and immediately began rubbing at the offensive white goo.

For a woman of her class, it seemed to Henry like it would be much easier to write a check than to do actual work in the trenches. So why would the Blue Violet volunteer and show such determination to come back every week. Was she really just curious about how the other half lived, or was she maybe trying to atone for the guilt of some past sin?

"I'll have to wear a different apron next time," the Blue Violet remarked soberly, finally giving up on the still-visible white tracking through her blue suit.

"Why?" Henry asked directly.

"Why, what?" she asked, confused. "Why do I need a different apron?"

"No, why are you here? Why will you be spending time one day a week helping feed the homeless?" Henry looked around the room with a grimace, and gestured to include everything, including himself. "I would think that for a woman like you, a different sort of charity work would be more desirable—a prettier charity, so to speak."

Henry wondered if he'd crossed the line. It really wasn't any of his business why and where this woman chose to volunteer. But in his day-to-day life, there was very little that grabbed his interest. And even less to make him feel valuable or important in any way. He was considered by most to be the dregs of society, and yet this beautiful gem from a different world had come to feed and provide for those such as him. He couldn't help but wonder why.

A spark lit in the Blue Violet's eyes, but it was not one of anger, but of understanding. Without a word, she reached down for her purse that was nestled at her feet. She unzipped it, pulled out a white envelope, and handed it to him.

"You can keep it," she said. "I have my own copy. I think it will explain things. Now you'd better eat your food before it gets completely cold."

Henry looked at her questioningly, while trying to balance his tray in one hand and examine the envelope in the other.

The Blue Violet gave a smile Mona Lisa would be proud of, and said simply, "It's just a Christmas card."

TODAY was a good day, Henry thought, feeling the warmth of the meek sun on his back as he walked the streets. In fact, on days like today, Henry could almost imagine that he was normal. Except for the fact that he didn't have a job, or a home, or anything of any worth to call his own. But he could almost fool himself into thinking that maybe he could get a job and at least one day be normal.

Then the memories would crowd in, reminding him of a reality where he was an old veteran haunted by ghosts of battle. They called it Post Traumatic Stress Disorder. But the way the doctors flung that and other terms around made Henry unsure of what was really wrong with him. Just thinking about it made the familiar hopelessness crowd close.

Henry began to tire of walking and looked for a corner where he could sit for a while. He wasn't as young as he used to be, and age seemed to make a few blocks take the same toll on his body that miles used to. Henry spotted a familiar alley and entered to find his usual spot in a corner by an old fire escape. He kicked away a pile of snow from where the protection of the overhanging buildings hadn't extended. Then he sat on the dry concrete, with his back braced against the brick of the building and his pack on the newly cleared spot beside him.

Sighing, he closed his eyes and just rested a moment.

Henry knew he'd been different after the war, but he'd managed to keep things together for his family. However, as he'd gotten older, it became harder to keep a grip on the memories, especially after Linda had enough and left him.

For years, medication and therapy kept things under control enough for him to work. He'd go through cycles where he'd truly believe he was cured only to have another, even worse attack of memories and panic. It would overwhelm him at times, and the bouts had only gotten worse when he'd lost his job. At his age, he'd likely have more of a chance of winning the lottery than getting another decent-paying job. His kids were grown; Linda had been gone for years. With no insurance and no one who seemed to care, Henry gave up on all treatment and life in general.

For about the thousandth time, the thought floated through his mind that he should try to call his son. But he hadn't talked to him since before he'd lost his apartment. Somehow, he just couldn't bring himself to admit to his son that he was homeless. He knew it was pride, but a father always wanted to be the man his son looked up to, no matter how old his child was. A mentally ill homeless man was not someone he'd ever wanted to be.

Idly, he dug in the pocket of his coat for the envelope the Blue Violet had given him. He then retrieved a stub of a pencil out of his pack and started drawing. Drawing often cleared the cobwebs from his mind, and every bit of paper Henry found was dedicated to his search for mental clarity.

It was actually a good sign that the memory of that little blue violet in the battlefield hadn't triggered another terrifying assault of memories. He'd even thought of it as a good memory, and for the first time in a long time, he felt a tingle of hope that maybe he was getting better.

But Henry knew he still had the night to get through. That good memory of a tiny flower could still trigger nightmares that would leave him shaking and screaming, only to wake to the weakness, depression and anxiety that would last days or longer.

Things hadn't been so bad in the summer, but this time of year, he had to stay in a shelter every night, and they were crowded, which didn't help the memories and choking panic that came with them. Thankfully, today was warm enough to be outside; he just couldn't sit still for long. When the temperature started to dip, he'd find a bed for the night, and then wake to do it all again tomorrow.

For several minutes, Henry just focused on each movement of his pencil, trying not to think beyond the weight of each stroke as it brought a black and white little flower to life. Soon the flower in the center of the envelope was surrounded by the darkness of debris and the charred remains of what was now unidentifiable. When the lead in Henry's pencil had transferred completely to the paper, Henry fished in his pack for another stub to finish his sketch.

Finally, he stopped, and looked at the black and white version of his poignant memory. Somehow, he felt better, as if the act of translating the scene to a scrap of paper had softened the emotion of it and turned it into something more palatable.

Feeling the cold seeping into his backside, he knew it was time to move on. He thoughtfully took out the typewritten paper from the newly-sketched envelope and glanced at it again. He'd already read it several times, but the idea only seemed to increase his depression. He wanted to do something meaningful; he wished he had something worth giving. But he was the lowest of the low. No earthly possessions. No employment. No money. No one to care. The only thing he actually had was a bunch of memories he wished he could forget!

Maybe that was part of his problem. He didn't feel like he could call his son because he didn't want to be a burden. He had nothing to offer in exchange for help. He could only bring grief.

Head down, Henry continued on his journey without a destination, trudging through the city streets.

Though he had a longing to make his own Christmas

card contribution, he was left feeling hopeless. If only he had some skill or talent that he could contribute.

He didn't suppose it had taken any special talent, skill, or even money for the Blue Violet to serve food for the homeless. He could probably volunteer to help for something like that, but that sounded too much like a job; he already knew he wasn't the dependable sort.

The drawing in his hand was proof enough of that. He used to have a good job as a graphic designer. He was an old-school designer. He didn't know much about the new technical stuff, but he'd been good enough at what he did that his company had kept him on. But when they'd faced cutbacks, they eventually had to let him go. He was a relic in a technological world. And that's what had begun his slide down to the hopeless muck that he was in now.

He had tried other jobs, but when not on his medication, there were days he just couldn't make it into work. The flashbacks left him weak and shaken, and the corresponding depression was like a suffocating blanket tied around his head.

No, he couldn't do anything that was job-like.

Henry sighed, lifting his head and hopelessly looking around at the people walking by, having no clue the misery housed inside an old, decrepit man. Nobody dared make eye contact with him. It was as if they saw right through him. In a city street packed with people, he felt completely alone and forgotten, and sometimes he wondered if God had forgotten him too.

He hadn't talked to God in months. Once upon a time, he'd been a believer. Deep down, he guessed he still was. He wasn't angry with God. One didn't spend his whole life believing one way and then stop because circumstances didn't go his way, but he was weary. He'd always believed that every person had a God-given purpose. But in the state he was in, he had trouble seeing his purpose, let alone the supposed greater plan God had for his life.

He used to think he had purpose. Even after Linda had left him, he'd continued to sing on a worship team, continued to trust that God would see him through the hard times. But along with everything else, Henry felt he'd lost God somewhere along the way.

Now, with a rich lady serving him lunch and giving him a Christmas card, he felt a strong longing for God and a desire to please and serve Him as she had done.

But how does one do that when there is nothing left?

Henry suddenly stopped dead still. People flowed around him, on their way to work or shopping, with to-do lists a mile long. He stood as if frozen, yet no one noticed; they just moved around him as if they were the current drifting around a rock in the stream.

After a solid minute, Henry stood up straight, took the cap off his head, and lifted his voice.

Chapter Seven

SHANTELL rubbed her red, gritty eyes and kept walking. She wasn't sure how much longer she could keep up the pace of going to school and working full time. Hopefully she would get some sleep after her last final tomorrow. If she could just make it until then. She'd just finished a long graveyard shift at an assisted living facility, followed immediately by a few hours of classes. Now she was on her way home to study and catch a couple hours of sleep before she had to get up tomorrow for her last day of finals before Christmas break.

Shantell suddenly heard the words to 'O Holy Night,' sang in a rich baritone. Her feet slowed as she looked around, trying to locate a car with Christmas music turned way up. But there was none, and she realized that the music she was hearing was completely a capella. She looked around for Christmas carolers, but it was just a single voice, which was strange when walking alongside a busy city street.

Finally, Shantell found the source. She walked forward, dazed, with her eyes glued with curiosity on a man with wild, steel-colored hair, a long gray beard, and old mismatched, dirty clothes. He looked like he was homeless, and yet his voice soared, making the shuffling feet, the sounds of conversation, and the business of traffic seem like complete silence.

The notes of the old hymn floated through the air with clear precision and were delivered as if he sang from his soul. It was the performance professional musicians always strive for because it really isn't a performance. It was a soul sharing truth and meaning through the translation of music. It was the lowest of society, sharing the depths of his soul in praise and inviting the world to witness.

By the time the man reached the third verse, tears flowed down his face as he sang.

"Truly He taught us to love one another…"

People still flowed past him, some with their heads down, not wanting to even make eye contact. A few gave nods of appreciation and moved on. Only Shantell and a few others stood still. There was something exquisitely beautiful about a man with nothing, offering all that was him in praise to his creator. As he reached the final chorus, the words and their meaning rang with such passion that Shantell didn't understand why the entire city didn't stand still, holding its breath at the gift that was being given.

"His power and glory evermore proclaim."

The last notes of the song were swept away in an echo off his lips, and with its fleeting breath, it escorted the moment with it. The few people who had stopped quickly resumed their journey.

The man opened his eyes, and his body completely deflated. The magic left, his shoulders slumped, and his gaze lowered to meet the sidewalk. He quickly replaced the stained baseball cap on his head and turned to shuffle away.

Still battling the burning behind her eyes, Shantell hurried forward. "Excuse me, sir." She rummaged in her wallet and pulled out a ten dollar bill. "Here, I'd like to give this to you. You have a beautiful voice. It was a blessing to hear you."

The man put his hand out to refuse the money. Shaking his head, he said, "No thank you, miss. I can't accept that. I didn't sing for money."

Shantell paused, completely shocked. Many people in the city made money as street performers. And this man obviously needed the money, yet he was refusing it. Why?

"I don't think I understand," Shantell said slowly. "I understand that you sang for everyone, but couldn't you still accept some payment from someone who enjoyed and appreciated it?"

The man silently, yet resolutely shook his head.

Now Shantell was even more curious. "Then why *did* you sing?"

The man pulled out a wrinkled envelope from his pocket. He took out the paper and read something. His lips moved as if he was memorizing a fact. Then he handed the paper and envelope to Shantell.

"Merry Christmas!" With a gentle smile and a tip of his worn cap, the man shuffled away.

SHANTELL sat on a park bench with a goofy smile on her face. What a romantic Christmas card!

When the homeless man had handed her the envelope she'd had no idea it would contain such a touching story. She read the letter through again, then flipped the envelope back over and looked at the detailed drawing of a flower. The homeless man must have drawn it, and the fact that she held something so personal, was touching as well.

Shantell stood, knowing she needed to hurry back to her apartment to get her studying done. She glanced back at the date and time listed on the card. She wanted to be there on Saturday to see what she hoped would be a beautiful, happy ending. She wasn't scheduled to work, so she was sure she could make it. But more than that, she wanted to be able to tell her part of the story. She would love to be able to share with the author of the card, Cole, about how his message had touched her through a homeless man singing beautifully on the street, but she also wanted to have her own link in the chain—to give a gift as it had been given to her, in every sense.

Shantell turned down her street and spotted her apartment ahead. Her roommate was working, so she should have the place to herself to study. But studying is not what she wanted to do. Maybe if she just had an idea of what kind of gift she could give, maybe then she would be able to focus on her work, get her final done tomorrow, and then carry out her plan.

Her mind flitted through possibilities, tossing them aside as soon as they bounced into her consciousness. Everything she could think of required money or a time commitment, neither of which she could give.

Finally, as she neared the entrance to her building, she blew her breath out in frustration, saying, "Fine, God. You put this Christmas card in my hand, so what would you have me do with it? What gift would you want from me?"

Laughter interrupted her thoughts. She turned to see a little girl dancing around in the snow, trying to pelt her mom with a snowball. The mother was far more accurate in her aim, and every time a snowball found its mark on the little girl's pink coat, she let out a squeal and giggled her way to find more ammunition.

To Shantell, the implication was uncomfortably clear.

"No, God," She immediately responded. "That wouldn't really be a gift. I want to do something for someone I don't know—someone less fortunate. Besides, I'm not the one who needs to apologize. She's the reason we don't have a relationship, not me."

A memory from her childhood popped into Shantell's head. She and her younger sister, Monique, had been staying at their grandma's house, when they'd started arguing, yet again. They were each insisting that the other one say sorry for the wrong they committed. Completely angry and frustrated, they had resorted to giving each other the silent treatment. Finally, Grandma had stepped in. "If you always wait for the other person to say sorry, then you'll soon be completely alone and never have a single person to talk to. Girls, you'll be a lot happier if you're the last to take offense and the first to say you're sorry."

"But it's her fault, Lord," Shantell argued, stubbornly refusing to apply the memory to her present situation. She's the one who decided not to see me. She is the reason we don't have a relationship."

So were you. And yet, I didn't stop loving and pursuing you.

Shantell shut her eyes. When she had been faithless, God had been faithful. When her world had fallen apart and she'd lost her sister, and then her mom, she had turned her back on God. But God hadn't given up on her, and gradually He had drawn her back to him. She had done the exact same thing to God that her mom had done to her. She had told Him to get lost, but He hadn't. He had kept reaching out, kept loving her, unwilling to let her go.

Shantell had been aware that her feet were moving, but she was so wrapped up in her own thoughts that she had no conscious thought of where she was going. Now she looked up and saw that she was no longer in front of her apartment. Instead, she was standing at a bus stop, and the bus was pulling up.

"Can I just think about it, God?" she silently begged. "Just give me a little time. I need to study. Maybe after my finals. Or maybe I could give some other gift for Saturday and deal with my mom later."

But the doors to the bus opened, and Shantell obediently got on. Some time on the drive, Shantell stopped begging to get out of her task. She, more than others, realized that tomorrow had no guarantee. When God told you to do something, you needed to do it right then.

So she rehearsed her speech. What would she say when

her mother opened the door? That was, *if* she opened the door. Shantell watched the passing lights of the city, mentally calculating the last time she's spoken to her mother. Monique had died a year ago. After four months of her mom blaming her for her sister's death, Shantell had left and hadn't gone back.

Eight months. She hadn't spoken to her mom in eight months, and her mom had made no effort to contact her. Shantell had kept in touch with her aunt, so she knew her mom was healthy; but a health report was all she'd ever asked her aunt for.

And it was better that way. At least, that's what she'd told herself. It was less painful. She didn't have the constant reminder and guilt. However, it wasn't until two months ago that she really felt like she'd started to heal. She'd tried to mask the pain in a variety of ways, but not until she'd turned back and let God bind up her wounds, had she begun to breathe without the oppressive weight of grief and guilt.

Now she knew what God wanted from her, and she didn't know if she could give it.

Shantell recognized her stop, and got off the bus as if on autopilot. She didn't pause to let the doubt and second thoughts catch up, but immediately started walking, her footsteps keeping rhythm as she alternated between desperately praying for strength and help, and rehearsing what she would say.

She turned down the street where she'd grown up and was bombarded by memories, but not the good ones. She saw again her mother's uncontrollable tears, heard her sobbing and saying that it was Shantell's fault that her sister was dead.

"You should have kept her with you," her mom accused. "She was only 16. You shouldn't have sent her home by herself!"

"I know, Mama," Shantell cried, kneeling beside where her mom sat inconsolable in a chair. "I was trying to protect her. I sent her home because the party was getting wild."

"Then why didn't you go with her!" her mom spat out. "You were a more experienced driver. If you would have been driving, maybe you could have swerved out of the way."

Shantell reached for her mother's hands, trying to offer the comfort of her touch and affection, but the angry woman pushed her away. She sighed, feeling completely heartbroken and weary. "I already told you a hundred times, Mama," she said softly. "I was trying to stay to help my friend at the party. She was drunk, and I didn't want her driving home. I was going to drive her, and then call Monique or you to run over and get me."

"So you traded your sister's life for your friend's."

"I didn't know a different drunk driver was going to hit and kill Monique!" Shantell protested. "If I had known, I wouldn't have let her go, or I would have driven her myself. I would have done any one of a thousand things to save her." Shantell paused, trying to work past her wavering voice to keep hold of the fragile control she held over her own sobs. "Mama, if I could go back and change it, I would. There's nothing you can say that I haven't already told myself. She was my little sister. I should have protected her, but instead, I sent her off to die. It's guilt that I will need to live with the rest of my life, but nothing I can do can bring her back for either one of us."

"You should have been the one to drive her home," her mom said stubbornly, as if she hadn't heard any of Shantell's speech. "If you would have been driving like you were supposed to, none of this would have happened."

"Mama, the other driver was drunk!" Tears streamed down Shantell's face. With hands outstretched, she begged her mom to listen to reason. "Monique wasn't killed because she made a driving mistake. If I had been driving, chances are I would have been killed!"

Her mom was silent. Completely silent.

But Shantell had never heard silence speak so much.

Shantell knew her mom was upset, and maybe she was thinking and implying things she didn't actually feel. Nothing had been right between them since Monique had died. This wasn't the first time they had discussed many of these issues, and Shantell had felt a suspicion that her mother put as much blame on Shantell as she did the drunk driver who had hit and killed Monique.

However, this was the first time Shantell had heard the words in her mother's silence.

Her mother blamed her for her sister's death, and nothing she could do would change that. Worse, Shantell clearly heard her mom's implication that it would have been better if she had been the one to die.

And maybe it would have been better. Monique had been the baby. She was sweet and easy-going. Their dad had left when Shantell was five, and much responsibility had been tasked to her, as the older child, at an early age. Maybe it was because of that added pressure and expectation, but Shantell had never seemed to be able to please her mom, at least not in the way Monique had.

Shantell looked into the angry, grief-twisted features of her mom's face and gave up. What relationship was there to salvage when your mom wished you dead?

So, with sobs choking her throat, she whispered, "Goodbye, Mom," and left.

She hadn't seen or spoken to her mom since then.

Now she stood in front of that same house she'd left eight months ago. All the indignation came flooding back, along with the hurt. She had been wronged, and yet God was asking her to lay the hurt in His hands and offer love and forgiveness to one who had shown no remorse.

With heart pounding and a sick feeling in her stomach. Shantell whispered a quick, simple prayer, "For you, my Lord."

Then she strode up the front steps and knocked on her mother's door.

Chapter Eight

"HAVE you heard from her, Helen?" Joanne asked into the phone, knots anxiously twisting in her stomach. "Is she okay?"

The voice on the other end of the line sighed. "Joanne, you really need to just call her and ask her yourself."

"I can't do that," Joanne said quickly, feeling the immediate panic at the thought. "I told you what happened—how awfully I treated her. She would never forgive me! And she shouldn't! You have no idea the terrible things I said to her!"

"I can imagine," Helen said dryly. "Remember, I'm your sister. I grew up with you."

"Yes, but she's my daughter, and yet I blamed her for everything and pretty much said I didn't want her. That I wished she was…" A sob caught in Joanne's throat, and she couldn't finish. Even after all these months, she couldn't think of what she had done and not feel overcome with shame and regret.

"You're right, Joanne, she's your daughter. Which means you need her and she needs you. You don't know what would happen if you tried to reach out to her. Even though you feel like you don't deserve forgiveness, she might feel differently. Like I said, you're her mom, and she needs you. Besides, it's Christmas! You can't let Christmas come and go without trying to make amends."

Joanne was quiet, thinking. Even though she longed to have her daughter back, she didn't feel like she had the strength to go to her and ask forgiveness. No parent should ever treat her child the way she had, and in her mind, she was unforgivable.

Obviously tiring of the silence, Helen sighed. "I haven't spoken to her in a couple of weeks. Last I knew, she was doing fine, but I know she is really busy. She has finals this week, and with working full time at that assisted living place, she probably isn't sleeping much."

"Thank you, Helen," Joanne said softly. She intended to tell her sister that she would think about what she'd said, but before she could get the words out, there was a knock at the front door.

"Gotta go, Helen," she said quickly, "Someone is at the front door, so I'll call you later."

Joanne hung up and hurried to answer the door. Being short, she had to stand on her tiptoes to look through the peephole. She saw a beautiful young woman with dark hair, and her heart leapt. But the image was so distorted through the narrow opening that she thought her eyes were deceiving her.

Wrenching open the door, she gasped at the sight of her daughter, and then couldn't release her breath.

"Mama, before you say anything, please let me talk first," Shantell said quickly. She stood stiffly, and her brow was furrowed anxiously. But Joanne didn't care.

All the air in her lungs released in a soft wail that was a strange mix of agony and utter joy. Without waiting for Shantell to say a single word, Joanne wrapped her arms around her daughter and held her as if she'd never let go.

She sobbed, smoothing her hair and murmuring, "My baby," over and over again. She felt Shantell's arms come around her, returning the embrace, and felt the wetness of Shantell's cheek against hers. And she sobbed all the harder.

Finally, she pushed back and held Shantell's face gently between her hands, lovingly studying her daughter's beautiful features and forcing her to meet her eyes.

"Listen to me, baby girl." Joanne's voice shook with intensity. "I was wrong. I said things I didn't mean and let you believe lies because I hurt so badly, I couldn't think clearly. I love you, always and forever. I always want you with me. I am so very thankful you were *not* in the car with Monique. I wouldn't trade your life for anything or anyone. You are alive, and that is the most precious blessing I have."

Shantell's body shook with great, heaving sobs.

Realizing that they were still standing on the porch, Joanne gently pulled her daughter inside the house and shut the door. She drew her to the couch, pulled her down, and held her as she had when Shantell was a little girl.

"I'm so sorry, Mama," Shantell hiccuped. "I should

have stopped her from going or just gone with her. She was my little sister, and I didn't protect her."

"Shh… It isn't your fault, Shantell. If you would have gone, you would have been killed as well. A man chose to get drunk and get behind the wheel. You are not responsible for his actions that took your sister's life."

After long minutes of speaking quietly and holding each other, the sobs of both women finally calmed.

"Mama, why didn't you call me," Shantell asked, no longer able to hold the question in. "If you wanted me back so bad, why didn't you come for me? It's been eight months!"

Joanne looked away. "I wanted to, but I couldn't. Shantell, I know how terribly I treated you. It has haunted my every waking moment since then. I didn't feel like you could ever forgive me. I didn't think I could even ask for your forgiveness because I didn't deserve it."

"Ask me," Shantell whispered. "Ask me now."

Joanne swallowed. "I am so sorry, baby girl. Can you please forgive me for blaming you and hurting you as no mom should do to a daughter?"

"Yes, Mama. I can forgive you, and I do."

Joanne hadn't thought she had any tears left, but at Shantell's words, her face crumpled once again, and she sobbed out the anguish of the past year. This time, Shantell was the one who held her.

Later, neither one of them felt like eating a big meal, but having a special treat together seemed the perfect way to celebrate the relief and lightness Joanne hadn't felt since losing her daughters. So they sat in the kitchen together, drinking hot tea and munching muffins.

"How did you know to come, Shantell?" Joanne asked, reaching across the table to squeeze her hand. "How did you know I needed you?"

Shantell smiled, but it was a smile that carried with it a sense of awe. She reached into her backpack and pulled out a wrinkled envelope. She set it down between them on the table, trying to carefully smooth out a pencil drawing on the front.

"I came because of a Christmas card."

JOANNE gently pulled the blanket up to her sleeping daughter's chin. She once again felt tears sting the backs of her eyes, but these were tears of joy. Her daughter was home!

Joanne reluctantly slipped quietly out of Shantell's room, trying to assure herself that her daughter would still be there in the morning.

They had spent a wonderful evening together. After talking, Joanne had helped Shantell study for her final. Thankfully, Shantell had brought all of her books and study materials in her backpack, and after the studying, Joanne was confident Shantell would do very well on the test tomorrow.

Thank you, Lord, Joanne breathed, with one last look at Shantell's sleeping form.

Joanne felt even more blessed that Shantell had agreed to stay the night in her old room instead of traveling back to her apartment. Tomorrow morning, Joanne would wake Shantell and take her to school, exactly as she'd done when her girls were little.

Joanne went back down to the kitchen and made herself a cup of chamomile tea. After everything that had happened, she wasn't yet ready to go to bed. As she sat drinking her tea, she felt more at peace than she had in the past year. But she still didn't feel whole. She didn't know that she ever would. Though one daughter had come back to her, her other daughter never would. It was as if a physical piece of her body was missing, and she didn't think she would ever not feel the agonizing loss of her child.

Joanne got up from the table, washed out her cup, and restlessly looked outside the window into the night. That nagging unsettled feeling hadn't seemed to go way either. Beneath the relief and joy of Shantell's return, beneath the grief of her loss, a deep anger still seethed. It was the same anger that had unjustly erupted at Shantell. But now, reason had prevailed and Joanne knew that hatred belonged solely to the one responsible for killing Monique. And that fierce, consuming emotion was the reason that, even though she'd been reunited with Shantell, Joanne was still not free.

Joanne couldn't deny that Shantell coming home had been miraculous. She walked back over to the table and hesitantly, almost reverently, touched the Christmas card that still lay there.

It was just a simple idea, written on a simple sheet of paper, yet it had been used by God to do a miracle in the lives of Joanne and her daughter. With so much that had been given to her, Joanne knew it was her turn. She felt an overwhelming longing to give a sacrifice of thanksgiving back to God, and be part of a miracle for someone else.

Holding the letter and flowered envelope gently in her hand, she took it into the living room and set it on the same couch where she had held Shantell a few hours before. Then she knelt down beside the couch. It wasn't a cathedral, it wasn't a church or even an altar, but Joanne needed to humbly ask to serve God.

She didn't bother with trying to come up with ideas. She didn't give God a multiple choice buffet of options. She just sincerely, wholeheartedly thanked God for bringing her daughter back to her arms, then whispered, "What would you have me do, Lord?"

An immediate, terrifying idea entered her head, and Joanne immediately tried to deny it as the answer she sought.

For what had been given to her was now being required.

Forgiveness.

"Dear, Lord, please. No. Anything but that!"

Chapter Nine

"SHANE, throw a shirt on. You have a visitor."

Shane stood from where he was doing pushups on the floor. He pulled on his orange, prison-issued shirt and waited while the guard unlocked the door to his cell.

At the guard's words, fear had sliced though Shane. He wasn't expecting a visitor. The only person who ever came to see him was his wife, Lisa. This wasn't her day to visit, so if she was showing up unexpectedly, that meant something was wrong.

If something had happened to one of the kids, he didn't know what he would do. He hadn't seen any of his five children in a year—by his choice. He'd told Lisa not to bring them. He didn't want his kids to see him this way. A daddy should be someone to look up to. It seemed like going to visit your dad in prison would be a good way to mess a kid up and traumatize him for life.

He wrote notes to his kids and talked with them on the phone, but it wasn't the same as getting to see and hold them. But he didn't have a solution, or even a long-term plan.

Something long-term was definitely what was needed. He was going to be in prison a long time. He likely wouldn't have a chance of getting out until his kids were adults, and yet he still wanted better for them than having a convict for a father.

He'd even told Lisa to not come, but she wouldn't listen. He'd told her to divorce him and find a good man who could be a father to their children, but she refused. Now she was here again, continuing to visit him despite his protests.

A few of the other prisoners called out as he and the guard passed their cells, but since most of them were flailing insults and jibes, Shane kept his head down and didn't respond. Even a year later, he still had trouble wrapping his mind around the reality that he was in prison. He usually went back and forth between intense grief and depression, and complete denial that this was his reality. Sometimes it seemed as if he was watching the nightmare of his life unfold from outside his body, and he couldn't make himself accept or feel that these horrible things were happening to him.

What he wouldn't give to go back and change that night a year ago!

He wasn't a bad person. He'd made mistakes before, and he really should have learned his lesson. But he'd been stupid. Despite Lisa's objections, he'd gone out partying with friends. They'd just been having a good time watching a big game at a sports bar. He really hadn't thought he was too drunk; he thought he could handle it. Besides, he didn't want to appear weak and have someone else drive him home. They were all drunk too!

The guard leading him stopped to talk to another guard about some issue with a prisoner.

Shane stood patiently, trying to tune out the echoes of sound in the prison. Oh, how he hated how everything echoed! It sounded so hollow and empty, an ever-present reminder of the hopelessness of his situation. There was nothing in sight except for more long days and years filled with those empty echoes, and all because of a single split-second that forever changed his life.

For the millionth time, he watched as his mind played out that night, and despite his agony, he was helpless to look away. It had all happened so fast.

He'd been rounding a corner when oncoming lights blinded him. He tried to blink away the disorientation only to have another set of lights blind him.

Then the impact.

He'd woken in the hospital with a couple broken bones and the news that he had killed a young woman. Charges were inevitable, especially when he had tested well-over the legal limit for alcohol.

There had been no point in pleading anything but guilty, though he'd gotten a lesser sentence than if the case would have gone to trial and he'd been found guilty. It wasn't his first DUI, which meant that he earned a very long prison sentence. Deep down, Shane couldn't fault the judge or dispute his punishment. He had killed a woman because of his own stupid choices. As bad as prison was, as horrible as it was to be away from his kids, the emotional trauma of those didn't compare to the tortuous guilt of knowing he had ended a life.

The guard finished his conversation, and he and Shane continued their journey to the visitors' area. Unfortunately, it wasn't as easy to walk away from his thoughts and self-incrimination.

Not for the first time in the past year, Shane thought of his mother's cookie jar. In so many ways, that memory from his childhood had come to symbolize his life.

One day, when his mom hadn't been looking, Shane had climbed up to get the cookie jar. Just as he held it in his hands and was about to lift the lid, the jar slipped and dropped to the floor, instantly shattering into thousands of tiny pieces. For Shane, time had stood still as he looked at the mess. His mind instantly denied what his eyes had just witnessed. The cookie jar had belonged to his grandmother and was his own mom's cherished possession; now it was completely destroyed at his hand. He longed to just run away, put his hands over his eyes, and pretend it hadn't happened.

But then, he heard his mom humming as she folded laundry in a different room.

He had to fix it! As irrational as it was, he stooped over the ceramic shards, hoping to piece it back together before his mom came. He scooped up a handful of the mess, only to have the pieces cut his hand as they fell back to the floor, completely useless.

On a horrible night, one year ago, Shane's life had shattered into a thousand pieces, destroyed in an act committed by Shane's own hand. He couldn't run, hide and pretend it hadn't happened, and as much as he wanted to, he couldn't pick up the pieces and put them back together.

The cookie jar had been whole and perfect, and then with a fraction of a second slip of the hand, it was destroyed. Same as his life. He'd had a beautiful wife and family, but now, in the blink of an eye, everything was destroyed and in pieces.

The screech of the door opening snapped Shane out of his thoughts. After the long walk through the cells, they finally left the echoes of the jeering inmates and the clanging of bars as Shane followed the guard to the visitors' meeting area.

Thankfully, the security at the prison still allowed him to meet in person with visitors. Even though he was terrified that Lisa was here to bring bad news, he still looked forward to holding her hand for a few minutes.

That was the only way he'd survived prison so far. If he thought about the future, he became hopeless and depressed. If he thought about the past and what he'd done, he was consumed by guilt and self-hatred. He could only survive one day at a time. And today, his wife was here to visit.

Shane was shown into the visitation room, and then was pointed to a table in the corner. He looked back at the retreating guard, thinking there was some mistake. The woman waiting at the table was not Lisa.

Then she turned, and Shane felt like he'd been punched in the gut. Shane didn't consciously move to the table, but he soon found himself seated across from the woman, unable to speak.

"Do you know who I am?" The woman asked, her lips tight and face tense.

Shane had instantly recognized the dark haired, older woman. Even though he would have given just about anything to forget, her face had been seared in his mind since the first time he'd seen her in the courtroom.

"Yes, ma'am," Shane managed. "You are Joanne Thomas. Your image has haunted my nightmares for the past year. I don't think I will ever forget your face or escape knowing what I took from you."

Shane swallowed. "I would give anything to go back and trade my life for your daughter's. I know an apology can ever make things better, but I am truly, very sorry."

Shane closed his eyes. No matter how many times he had imagined apologizing to Joanne Thomas, he had never thought he'd actually ever have the chance to do it in person. Now in reality, it sounded just as trite as it had in his head. How could "sorry" ever hope to communicate the depth of his sorrow.

Now he braced for what he was sure was the storm to follow. He had killed her daughter, and whatever verbal lashing she had to give, Shane knew he deserved it all and more.

Silence stretched so long that Shane finally chanced a glance up. Mrs. Thomas was studying him calmly, but the flickers in the depths of her dark eyes gave no clue as to her thoughts.

"Relax, Mr. Jackson," she said finally. "I am not here to spew hate, lecture you, or tell you how much you took from me. I somehow have the feeling you already know."

Confused, Shane met her gaze fully for the first time. The look on his face must have made it obvious that he was expecting her anger and hatred. But after she paused for several seconds, showing no indication of offering an explanation, Shane quietly ventured, "Then why did you come?"

Joanne took out an envelope and set it on the table between them. "To give you a Christmas card."

"DO you believe in God, Mr. Jackson?"

Shane had stared, completely dumfounded for so long that Mrs. Thomas had gotten a far away look. Then she'd abruptly shot off a question that gave Shane whiplash with the sudden subject change, confusing him all the more.

Joanne Thomas had come to give him a Christmas card?

Shane shook his head as if to clear it. "No, ma'am," he said, finally answering her question. "I don't believe in God."

"Why not?" she asked bluntly.

"Because I figure it doesn't really do me any good to believe in God." God was a subject that was off-limits in Shane's own mind. But Joanne wasn't going to be satisfied with a simple answer, so with his voice strained, Shane felt forced to fully explain his position. "I'm not the type of person who goes to heaven. Whether I believe in God or not, I'm destined for the same fate. I'm the faceless villain everyone warns their kids about—a person terrible and stupid enough to get behind the wheel when he was drunk and killed someone innocent. Like I said, any God that exists doesn't have a lot to offer me."

Shane released his breath in a rush, trying to manage his emotions. Seeing Joanne Thomas and discussing God only intensified his self-hatred. "Is that why you're here, then—to preach at me?"

Mrs. Thomas snorted. "Goodness, no! I came to tell you I forgive you, and to give you the Christmas card, of course."

"What do you mean? Is this some kind of religious thing you have to do?"

Joanne's eyebrows lifted in surprise. "Have to do? No. You see, it may surprise you to know that you and I aren't so different. Like you, I did something terrible. I hurt someone and didn't think I ever deserved anything more than hate. Then, when I thought it was impossible, I was offered forgiveness. I didn't deserve it, I could in no way earn it, and yet it was given freely. And it occurred to me that I had been given what I myself had been unwilling to give. How could I accept God's forgiveness, or anyone else's, when I could not forgive you."

"'For everyone who has been given much, much will be demanded,'" Shane said thoughtfully.

"Luke 12:48," Joanne said with surprise.

"I may not be a believer, but my wife is," Shane said with a shrug. "She gave me her Bible. That was a verse she had highlighted. There's not a whole lot of entertainment to choose from in prison."

Joanne nodded. "Let me make something clear, this was not a superficial, quick decision so I can mark it off my Sunday School homework list. Nor has it been easy. I have wrestled with it for days and now am right up against the

Christmas card deadline."

Joanne paused, then looked him straight in the eye with all sincerity. "I can't forget that my daughter is dead because of your actions. You haven't done anything to earn forgiveness, but neither have I. As I received mercy and grace, I'm now offering it to you. Here and now, I give up my right to be angry and hateful toward you. I don't count your debt against me. It is as if it has been paid in full. So, that is what I mean when I say Shane Jackson, I… forgive… you."

The whole time Mrs. Thomas was speaking, Shane studied her, looking for some trace of deceit, bravado, or anything that would indicate she was putting on a show. There was none. Then her final words pierced the wall of protection he had carefully constructed around himself, and he felt their meaning to the depths of his being.

He gasped for breath as silent, sobs began shaking his body.

It was undeserved. He was a sinner, and she had been his victim. He deserved her wrath and unforgiveness, but he had found love and mercy instead.

He had never thought forgiveness was a possibility for him, and now, suddenly, he had it, having done nothing to earn it.

As his shoulders heaved under the weight of emotion, he felt Mrs. Thomas come around the table and wrap her small arms around Shane's frame. Together, they sobbed, both for the grief they had shared and now the healing.

After long minutes, Mrs. Thomas pulled away, but kept hold of one of Shane's hands, squeezing it gently. It was time for her to go. She smiled warmly, though her eyes were still red and puffy from tears, and promised that she would come back to visit.

With her free hand, she picked up the white envelope still sitting on the table, and carefully placed it in Shane's open palm. Then she wrapped his fingers around it.

Then, with a cheerful, "Merry Christmas!" she turned and left.

Chapter Ten

"IS this the last one?" Cole asked as he hefted the basket into his arms.

"No," Sarah answered, checking her list. "I'm pretty sure we have one more after this.

Cole set the basket down and tried to peer around the empty boxes littering the back of the truck. He reached out and moved one aside, finally locating the missing basket stuffed with food and other items for a family in need.

"You're right. There's one more here," he said, stifling a groan as he looked at his watch. It was the big day. Christmas Eve. He had to meet everyone in the park at 2:00. But if Sarah had her way, they might be competing with Santa's late night delivery schedule.

"What's the matter?" Sarah quipped. "Are you feeling

your Scrooge?"

"No. But after delivering fifty Christmas cheer baskets, I am beginning to relate to the Grinch."

The first ten or so baskets had been fun. Thankfully, Cole had successfully managed to smooth things over after last week's disaster. After he had met Sarah at the Jacksons and helped out, he and Sarah had stayed up late talking. It seemed that, as far as Sarah was concerned, everything was forgotten. The incident had been a slight speed bump hardly worth slowing down for.

But Cole had felt a bigger emotional investment in the failed dinner date, and he still carried around some unease.

He didn't want to lose Sarah. He felt like he'd come close with his stupid actions, and now he appreciated being with her all the more. Even through today's endless deliveries of Christmas baskets, he had thoroughly enjoyed getting to spend time with her.

It had been wonderful to see the looks on people's faces and feel that they had truly made a difference. But Cole hadn't realized how many families had been on Sarah's list. He had worked yesterday and hadn't been there when Sarah's crew had done the assembly of all the donated food, gifts, and other items for the Christmas baskets. He had volunteered to help with the delivery Christmas Eve morning. However, after the tenth basket, he had begun to worry that this project was going to run into his 2:00 appointment at the park.

"It hasn't been fifty, just eighteen," Sarah clarified, after carefully consulting her list.

"So far." Cole shot back. "You'll probably run into a few more needy people between now and when we drop off basket number 19. Then we'll have run to the store and restock."

"No, that won't happen." Sarah said firmly. "After assembling and delivering 19 baskets, we've done our duty. Besides, I told you we could spend the afternoon together, and I intend to keep that promise."

"I'm glad to hear that," Cole said, planting a kiss on her bent head as he passed. "Skeptical, but glad to hear it."

Sarah made a face at him. "Just get the box up the stairs, Mr. Grinch."

"See, that's the only reason you like me," Cole showed off his best pout. "I'm just here for physical labor; I'm the muscle."

"No, but that's a definite plus!" Sarah quipped. "I also keep you around for your cheery disposition."

A ring of the doorbell and an overjoyed single grandma and grandchildren later, Cole and Sarah got back into his truck. Cole listened to Sarah give him directions, and chanced another glance at his watch.

12:00.

If this didn't take very long, they could still make his plans work. Sarah had promised to spend the afternoon with him, ending with dinner at her family's house. He should have learned from his last failed date, but in spite of himself, he had made plans. Just a few, he'd told himself, and ones that could easily be adjusted or canceled if necessary. Two o'clock marked the only event that was set in stone.

Cole slid a glance at Sarah as they stopped at a light. Did she suspect anything? She hadn't acted any differently than normal. But after Cole heard that a news program had featured a quick segment called 'Have you received your Christmas card?' he'd been worried that Sarah would find out about his project. It still amazed him that his card had been featured on the news, and from the few people who had mentioned the card to him, it sounded as if there might be a good turnout for the main event.

He supposed that it would be wonderful if just one person had given a gift of kindness. He was sure that would be enough to be worth it. But part of him hoped for at least a few stories he could share with Sarah. All week he'd alternated between excitement and outright fear and remorse. Many times he'd felt like an idiot for sending out that card. The idea he thought had been great a week ago, often sounded stupid and cheesy. In the light of day, it didn't seem realistic to expect his card to inspire people to action and make a difference. So whenever he felt the panic grip him, he tried to pray, asking that God be the one in charge of his project and make something beautiful out of his effort.

"Cole, I need to tell you something," Sarah said, drawing him out of his thoughts.

His immediate response was fear, and after glancing over and seeing Sarah's telltale nervous habit of repeatedly tucking her hair behind her ears, Cole was even more nervous. "Okay," he said cautiously.

"I'm sorry," Sarah paused, trying to manage her emotions while Cole was left to wonder what on earth she was apologizing for.

Taking a deep breath, she continued. "You were right last week at the restaurant. I need to slow down and delegate some of my responsibilities to others. I still don't think I'll be able to leave my cell phone. I know there are times when there's an emergency, and I need to be the one to go. But,

I'm going to try to do a better job of involving others and setting aside time when I'm off duty."

Cole was surprised. He'd never expected Sarah to apologize or change her behavior. He had assumed that he was the one who needed to come to terms with the fact that Sarah's dedication to her job and helping others was part of who she was, and he was ready to make whatever sacrifice he needed in order to love her. It would be wonderful if she was truly willing to meet him halfway, but he wanted to make sure she was doing it for the right reasons, and not just for him.

"Sarah, I know your job is important, and you know I apologized already for getting upset with you last week. I'm willing to accept you however you are, though it would be really nice to spend more time with you away from your job. But I don't want this to be about me. I want this to be a conviction that you feel is something God wants of you. Can you tell me what made you decide to let others take some of the work?"

Sarah smiled. "Don't worry, Mr. Grinch. It isn't about you at all. As I was thinking and praying about it this week, I realized that part of the reason it's difficult for me to give any of my charity work to someone else is because I like it so much. I want to be the one who gets to help others, to see the looks on their faces, and to know I helped make a difference. Then I realized how selfish that was. There is a blessing in being able to give and help others, and I need to allow other people to feel and receive that blessing."

Cole pulled up to the curb in front of a small house in need of paint, and shut off the engine. He reached over, took Sarah's hand and lifted it to place a gentle kiss on the back.

She gently smiled back at him, and Cole was

overwhelmed with love and wonder for Sarah Whitman. Though no words were spoken, there was a connection that went deeper than anything that could be verbalized. Once again, Cole was flooded with the certainty that he wanted Sarah to be his wife.

Out of the corner of his eye, Cole saw the front door to the little house open and a child step out to look at them curiously. The spell broken, Cole and Sarah stepped out of the truck to make their last delivery.

Delivery number 19 went smoothly, and Cole and Sarah soon left the little house with seven happy residents. As they walked down the cracked sidewalk hand-in hand back to his truck, Cole looked at his watch with satisfaction. They still had time to get some lunch and then meet the horse-drawn carriage that would take them to the park. He nervously fingered the small box in his jacket pocket. It really was going to happen! He hoped Sarah would like the surprise of the carriage ride. He'd packed a few blankets in the back of his truck, just in case the ride was cold. Then, even if there was nobody there to meet them at the park, Cole would make his proposal.

Cole opened the truck door for Sarah, and stepped aside to let her in.

The ringing of her cell phone made her pause.

"Hello?" She said, answering.

Cole couldn't hear the conversation, especially since Sarah just listened, but he saw when her eyes lit up with excitement.

"Yes!" she said enthusiastically. "When?" She looked down at her watch. "Okay, I can be there in twenty minutes. Thank you!"

She hung up and turned to Cole with sparkling eyes. Then, suddenly, as if realizing what she'd just agreed to, the spark disappeared as if a candle being blown out by the breeze.

She looked at her phone, then back to Cole. "Cole, I'm so sorry!"

And Cole knew. No horse-drawn carriage.

Cole took Sarah's free hand in his. "It's okay. Just tell me where Superwoman needs to rush off to and when I can have her back."

Sarah nodded, her lip trembling slightly. "My car is parked at the church. I need you to drop me off there. I've been trying to get some publicity. Then they just called and said they could fit me in right now if I could make it to the station. I can't turn down this opportunity!"

"I understand. We'd better hurry then." He urged Sarah into the truck, and shut the door. Then he hurried to his own side.

Sarah often did radio, and sometimes television, interviews promoting the charitable work she was in charge of. Such publicity was great for incoming donations and new volunteers. Cole understood that she couldn't turn down something like that.

By the time Cole dropped Sarah off, they'd decided that she would call him when she was done with the interview. Then she'd catch up with him wherever he was.

Maybe he should have told her everything, but there wasn't time. With a quick kiss, she was out the door and gone, and Cole was left with his mind scrambling for a back up plan.

He mechanically went to Subway and got a sandwich, but even after he ate, he hadn't had any epiphanies. There was nothing he could do. He still hoped that Sarah would be done before 2:00, but from experience, he knew that these types of things were like overtime in a game. There was a vast difference between the time on the clock—the amount of time it was supposed to take—and the reality of the amount of time it actually took. If Sarah thought it would take an hour, Cole better double that estimate.

After eating, Cole decided he had nothing better to do than go wait at the park. He sat on a bench near the amphitheater and watched squirrels fight over a piece of litter. But he wasn't really seeing the squirrels, he was praying and rehearsing in his mind what to say when a bunch of people came to see a proposal and the potential bride didn't show up.

He would just have to be honest and tell them that the same beautiful, giving heart that had prompted him to write the Christmas card, had called Sarah away again to help others. Then, if anyone had a story to share, maybe they could tell everyone.

Cole lifted his head, shutting his eyes in prayer as he felt the cold brush past. Though blue sky spanned from horizon to horizon, the temperature wasn't above freezing, and the steady breeze likely dropped it a few more degrees. A couple inches of snow tightly packed the ground like a crisp, white blanket. Even though the snow wasn't in danger of melting, hopefully the cold would at least be bearable for anyone who came.

The more he thought about it, the more he was sure he could come up with something to salvage the meeting of people here in the park, no matter how large the group.

Unfortunately, he didn't have that same confidence about his proposal. This would be his second attempt at a proposal. He pretty much had nothing left. He had tried to make it special and romantic; he had tried to do something to let Sarah know that he understood her and loved her. However, right now, he was leaning toward dropping to his knee the next time he saw her! He wanted to marry her, and never mind the surroundings or the circumstances. The only thing that mattered was her 'yes.'

"Are you here about the Christmas card," a rough voice said, interrupting Cole's thoughts and scaring away the squirrels.

"Yes," Cole answered, standing to see an old, grizzled man. He was wearing worn clothes in layers and carried a backpack. By his general appearance, Cole guessed that he was probably homeless.

"Good," the man nodded. "That's why I'm here."

Cole was going to question the man a little more, but he saw several other people milling around the amphitheater. A mom with some kids, an older lady in a skirt and fancy hat, and a few others who had their backs to Cole.

Cole took out his phone, but there were no new notifications. Sarah hadn't called. And it was just a couple minutes before 2:00.

Reluctantly, he walked over to the center of the amphitheater. He stood on the concrete stage area and looked out across the snowy slope. There weren't very many people here. In the back of Cole's mind, he had expected more, especially with the news story. He didn't even see Sarah's family. He'd really taken a risk in letting them in on his plan, and unfortunately, it looked as if he'd pay the price of opening himself up like that.

Oh, well, as he'd said, if that card had touched one person, then it was worth it, even if his family and friends didn't even show up!

Even though his audience was sparse, he still felt slightly nauseated and dizzy, like he'd run too fast for too far.

Cole looked at his phone one last time: 2:03 and quite silent.

Ignoring the sick feeling in his stomach, Cole cleared his throat. "I want to thank you all for coming. Unfortunately, we've had a slight change of plans…"

Cole's voice trailed off. Movement at the top of the hill surrounding the amphitheater caught his eye. Then the entire crest was swarmed as people descended into the little valley. Lots and lots of people.

Cole's mouth fell open in shock. The area was soon filled with so many people you couldn't see the snow beneath their feet. And they kept coming. Crowding in and spilling past the edges of the stage and the amphitheater itself.

Strangely, with that many people, you would expect there to be noise, but there wasn't. Everyone was silent, with all eyes trained expectantly on Cole.

Before he could gather his wits and speak, he noticed a disturbance to his left. Like the parting of the Red Sea, people turned aside, creating a tunnel.

Sarah Whitman emerged.

Chapter Eleven

WITH a joyful, slightly mischievous smile stretching her face, Sarah walked up and joined Cole onstage.

"Hi!" she said casually.

"Hi," Cole replied cautiously, feeling very confused. Were all of these people here about his Christmas card? People continued to pack into the area in more numbers than Cole could count. And what was Sarah doing here? "I thought you were supposed to call me!"

"I'm sorry," she said seriously, "but I was busy hijacking your plans."

Wordlessly, Cole stared at her, now even more nervous and confused. As they stood looking at each other, more and more people filed in, standing shoulder to shoulder in a widening expanse in front of the stage.

Sarah held her hand out to him, and he automatically took it. With her other hand, she lifted a typed paper. "I hope you don't mind, I brought my own copy."

"You already know." It wasn't a question. But with the realization, all of Cole's hope deflated like a balloon, and was quickly replaced by embarrassment and disappointment. All that work... and his proposal was ruined.

Sarah nodded. "I have a confession to make. The interview I had wasn't about the charity. It was about you. I wanted to turn the tables on you a bit. I asked everyone who had received a Christmas card to meet me on the other side of the park to help me with something. That interview, less than two hours ago, gained a lot more attention to the project. Look around you, Cole. See what you've done—how many lives you've touched? How could I not know?"

Following Sarah's gesture, Cole looked out at the sea of people. While they talked, the amphitheater had completely filled with people lined up and stretching out the sides beyond Cole's field of vision. He looked out, now recognizing the beaming faces of Sarah's family standing front and center along with a group of friends. He also saw several of the families Sarah had been helping through her charity work, including Lisa Jackson and her five grinning kids.

Cole turned back to the woman who had started it all. "Sarah, the credit isn't mine; it belongs to you." Cole took out his own copy of the Christmas card, the original, from where it had been neatly folded in his coat pocket. "I know you've already read it, but if it's okay, I'd like to read it to you myself."

Sarah nodded, her eyes not leaving his. "I wouldn't have

it any other way."

Cole lifted his voice to reach the audience that had begun to grow restless. They had come here for an event, and watching Cole and Sarah talk quietly didn't quite fit the billing. "I know everyone here is probably already familiar with the Christmas card I wrote a week ago, but please bear with me as, in my own words, I tell Sarah why we are here today."

He began reading, his voice rising clearly over the large, still audience.

Dear Friends and Family,

I love Sarah Whitman. And I need your help.

Sarah is the most beautiful, wonderful, generous person I have ever met, but because of my own foolish mistakes, I find myself in the position where I need to prove my love to her. I want to show her I love her in a way that also demonstrates that I understand who she is.

Sarah helps people. No task is beneath her if it involves helping someone else. I now understand why she is so passionate about helping others. As she told me, she doesn't do it for other people. Instead, she does it for God.

Sarah chooses to help the "least of these." In every person she rescues, in every toilet she cleans, in every good deed she performs, she is doing it for God.

This Christmas season, I wanted to send a card that was meaningful, and when thinking about Sarah, I realized something I'd never thought about before.

When Jesus was born, He came with none of the ceremony He deserved. Here was God incarnate, the creator of the world, and yet no one realized fully who He was or that He came with the purpose to save those who couldn't save themselves. Throughout his life on Earth, He faced ridicule and unbelief, and was never recognized for who He was. Then He died at the hands of those He had come to save.

We have the benefit of hindsight. We can read the Bible and see the scope of His life, from birth, to death, to resurrection and ascension, all laid out in a few chapters. We can acknowledge what He did for us, repent, and accept his salvation and Lordship in our lives. But somehow, that never seems like quite enough for the One who was born to die the death I sinfully deserved.

That got me thinking. What if, on that first Christmas day, the world had recognized its Savior had come? What if I'd had the opportunity to be there, to join the Magi in bringing gifts to the baby who would pay the price for my sins? What gift would I have brought?

Is it too late? That same baby, that same Savior, is alive today. What if I could give Him a gift. He has given me so much, yet what possible token could I give to show my love? What do you give the One who owns it all? What would He want?

I believe my Sarah has already figured it out. Jesus said, "Truly I tell you, whatever you did for one of the least of these brothers and sisters of mine, you did it for me." Matthew 25:40, NIV

So when Sarah helps others-when she gives of her time, spends her own money, moves mountains to meet need, or even cleans someone else's toilet-she is not doing it for that person. To her, it is as if she is doing it for Jesus. Sarah's attitude is one of joy because she would feel privileged to do those things for her Savior. To her, it is as if Christ himself is in need. She cleans because she sees Christ instead of the old couple who can't clean for themselves. Instead of the homeless man who needs a meal and a shower, she sees that Jesus is hungry and dirty. The family who needs a roof over their heads hold a special place in her heart, but she still is helping provide for their needs because Jesus is the one who needs shelter.

So what about me? To give a gift Christ would value, I should care for one of the "least of these" with the attitude that I was doing it directly for Him.

What about you? If you were to give a gift to Jesus, what would it be?

Sarah's life and actions are a testimony. I want her to know that I understand her and value her life's work, but I also want her to realize the tremendous influence she has. You see, Sarah also doesn't value material gifts. The kind of gift I want to give her is one that magnifies her life's work and testimony. And I need your help.

This Christmas, please prayerfully consider what kind of gift you would give Jesus. If you could meet Him face-to-face, what would you present to him? If you decide to do as Sarah, and help one of the "least of these" as unto the Lord, then I would be very grateful if you would meet me at London Park at 2:00 in the afternoon, Christmas Eve. Sarah and I would both love to hear of your Christmas gift to God. Maybe if Sarah hears what influence she's had, and understands that I value the woman she is, maybe, just maybe, she'll allow me to be her partner in life as her husband. On that Christmas Eve afternoon, with a host of the "least of these" in witness, maybe Sarah Whitman will say yes.

Sincerely,

Cole Nikols

P.S. One last favor. I am sending this Christmas card to all the people I know, but if you could pass it on to others, I would appreciate it! Let's see how many Christmas presents we can give Jesus!

Cole finished. He could hear his own heart beating in the stillness of everyone holding a collective breath. Without pause or hesitation, Cole knelt down on one knee. He took out the little box from his pocket and opened it. He looked up at Sarah, his eyes wide open with sincerity and love.

"Sarah, I love you. I love you for who you are, including your heart for God and your dedication to serving others in His name. All of these people are here because of a message based on your life and testimony. I want to share that with you. I want to love God and serve Him right beside you. Sarah Whitman, you are the most beautiful, wonderful woman I have ever met. Will you do me the honor of allowing me to be your husband?"

His speech over, he waited without breathing, his upturned eyes never leaving Sarah's tear-streaked cheeks and sparkling blue eyes.

With a tremulous smile, Sarah spoke in a quiet voice that somehow carried to every person watching, "Look around you, Cole!"

Startled, Cole's gaze swerved to the audience he had almost forgotten existed.

Each person was holding up a sign. Each sign had three large letters.

Y-E-S

Cole's eyes swung back up to Sarah, looking for confirmation.

She held her own small, matching sign, wonderfully labeled *Yes*.

With her face wreathed in an almost shy joy, Sarah said with certainty, "I wanted to be sure you understood that my answer was a thousand times, 'yes.'"

Cole let out a whoop and jumped up. Grabbing Sarah, he lifted and whirled her around in a complete circle. Then he set her feet back on the concrete and kissed her soundly to the music of clapping and cheering.

Finally coming up for air, he accused. "This is what you needed their help with?"

Sarah shrugged. "Well, I couldn't say 'yes' a thousand times myself! Besides, I also got to hear some of the Christmas card stories a little early. Cole you won't believe how far of a reach your message has had—how God has used it to bring great blessings to people's lives. I've heard everything from countless acts of generosity, to incredible stories of forgiveness. A reporter told me the card was even going through a prison! Cole, wherever it goes, miracles follow!"

Feeling the shock and disbelief of the moment, he raised his voice once again. "Sarah and I want to hear your Christmas card stories. If you are not able to stay, please write it down and send it to us. If you have the Christmas card, I believe I listed my contact information at the bottom."

His eyes filtered through the crowd, landing on people with cameras marked with TV station logos. Cole knew the story of the Christmas card had to be told in a way that included all the stories and gifts that had been inspired by it. Knowing what needed to be said, he raised his voice again.

"If everyone here has a story, then we have work to do. The important thing is to tell your stories to others. Don't let the blessings God has poured out fall asleep before they are shared. And keep the gifts going. If you have received a blessing, it isn't too late to take your turn at giving."

When the applause died down, Cole spoke his final words. "And now, if you'll excuse me, I have a few things I need to address with my soon-to-be wife!"

With a wave and a 'Merry Christmas,' Cole turned back to Sarah, gathered her into his arms, and kissed her.

Great cheers filled the amphitheater once again, but Cole tuned them out. He kissed her as if for the first time, knowing that if he had a kiss to match every one of her thousand yes's, it wouldn't be enough to last a lifetime with Sarah.

Moving his left hand to better hold the woman he loved, Cole unconsciously let the Christmas card slip from his fingers. With everyone excitedly talking and sharing stories of changed lives, no one noticed as the sheet of paper was carried away on the winter breeze, guided by the breath of God to find its next recipient.

I find it amazing when God asks me to live out the message of one of my books. So now it's my turn to tell my personal story of how the message of The Christmas Card has been lived out in my life.

When I was a child, my family's church took up an offering so that I could have the surgery that would save my vision. I was on the receiving end of a gift that changed my life. Fast forward many years, and I wrote a book, called *The Christmas Card*. While writing it, my family had the opportunity to sacrifice, giving a gift to our Lord through blessing a family in need. Rather fittingly, we were able to help the family get their child some much-needed medical care that he might have otherwise not received. In that instance, I got to be on the giving end.

From the beginning, my vision for this book was

simple—that it be a Christmas card that people could send to their friends and family. However, I also realize this type of project hasn't been done before, and therefore needs a little help. The greatest book ever written would never sell any copies if no one knew about it!

So I'm asking, especially if you read the book and enjoyed it, that you help me spread the word. As always, great reviews are helpful, but I also encourage you to send the book and its message to those on your Christmas list and share your excitement about it with others.

During the Christmas season, *The Christmas Card* ebook will be available wherever ebooks are sold, and be priced at 99 cents. Giving a gift of an ebook is as simple as pushing the "Give as a Gift" button on Amazon and filling in an email address. The paperback, priced as low as I can make it, will also be available on Amazon, christianbook.com, and possibly other retailers if requested. For more specific details, information, and ideas, please visit my website amandatru.com (link below).

If you have any great ideas or opportunities for sharing about the project, please contact me. For instance, if you know of a pastor who would appreciate sharing or even using the book in a study, please let me know, and I may be able to arrange to have a review copy sent. I'm always thrilled to answer emails, do interviews, and even speak at events, if at all possible.

Finally, I ask for prayer. What I really want most is that the message of this book be told and have the chance to help others, serve God, and bring glory to Him.

I can testify from personal experience of the life-changing blessings of being on both receiving and giving ends of a gift. I want to be that person who serves

God by blessing others.

Oh, that *The Christmas Card* could have other real life testimonies as wonderful as the one portrayed in the story!

AS you probably already know, this book was designed as a Christmas card that would deliver an inspirational message through a great story.

The verses and themes in this book are ones that I have wrestled with myself, which has produced a message that is very personal. For instance, years ago, I was an exhausted mommy taking care of my own kids, when I also started caring for another toddler as a way to help his parents. Though I absolutely adored him and was happy to be able to help, sometimes the sheer lack of sleep and the never-ending diapers became a bit overwhelming.

One day, I was changing the little guy's diaper with my bad attitude firmly in place. Suddenly, a verse popped into my mind. *"Truly I tell you, whatever you did for one of the least of these brothers and sisters of mine, you did for me."* Matthew 25:30, NIV

And the verse became real. It was as if God was saying, if I was that baby laying there needing a new diaper, what would your attitude be? As strange and rather humorous it is to think of God as needing a diaper change, the thought completely changed my perspective. And I realized the true meaning of a verse I had heard my whole life. We are to serve others as if they aren't "others," but God himself. The acts of service I would joyfully do if my Lord was in need, I should, by the same measure, do for the "least of these." My love for God should be the motivation for all of my good works, as if they are unto Him.

My prayer is that, as you discuss the book, you will be collectively and individually inspired to serve God, considering the same questions Cole posed in his letter and applying them to your life. May you look upon your service in a new light, and find a new joy in knowing you get to love God through it.

In short, it is your turn.

You have received the Christmas card from your dear friend, Amanda. Now, what will you do with it?

1. What did you find inspiring in *The Christmas Card*?

In the book, the Christmas Card travels through the hands of multiple, very different people, changing their lives in unexpected ways.

1 Peter 4:10-11

2. Discuss the gifts each person in the story gave. Which of the gifts would you have found more difficult to give?

3. What was your favorite part of the book?

4. Whose story did you relate to most?

5. Was there one of the stories that you found most touching or inspiring?

Several Bible verses acted as themes in the book. For instance, "as you did it to the least of these, brothers, you did it to me."

Matthew 25:37-40

6. I shared in the beginning of this Readers' Guide what this verse meant to me, as applied to my life. What does it mean to you? What have you seen or experienced about doing something as unto the Lord?

7. How should doing something unto the Lord change your attitude?

Another influential verse in this book is, *Everyone to whom much was given, much will be required.* (Luke 12:48b) For Joanne, that meant forgiveness.

Luke 12: 35-48, John 1:12-14, 1 Samuel 12:24, 1 John 3:17-18

8. How do you see this as applying to your own life? What blessings has God given you? Is there a way you can pass the blessing on to others?

9. Have you ever been given an undeserved act of kindness? Have you ever been the recipient of an act of charity or gift that made a difference in your life?

10. What experiences have you had being on the giving and receiving ends of generosity?

Proverbs 19:17

11. Is there a blessing in giving unto the Lord? Is there a blessing in giving to others? What do such blessings looks like?

Acts 20:35, Proverbs 11:25, Luke 6:38

Please reread Cole's letter, as he himself read it in the last chapter.

Now it's your turn.

Philippians 2:1-11

12.Can you brainstorm different ways you can help people you know as unto the Lord? Think of both big and small ideas.

13.What do you think God wants from you? If you were to give Him a gift, what would it be?

Matthew 5:16, Hebrews 13:16

NOTES:

_____

_____

_____

_____

_____

_____

_____

_____

_____

_____

_____

_____

_____

_____

_____

IF you enjoyed reading *The Christmas Card*, be sure to check out even more great books by Amanda Tru.

Stand-Alone Novels:
Secret Santa

The Romance of the Sugar Plum Fairy

Random Acts of Cupid

The Assumption of Guilt

The Tru Exceptions Series:
Book 1: Baggage Claim

Book 2: Point of Origin

Book 3: Mirage

PLEASE enjoy this brief excerpt from *Secret Santa*, available wherever fine books are sold.

IT was time for Hailey Rhodes to admit the truth: things were not going well. She was broke, currently dressed as a Christmas elf, and Santa Claus was hitting on her.

Hailey glanced down at her watch. Ugh! Her shift wasn't going to be over for another four hours!

"Am I really that boring, or do you have some place you have to go?" Santa asked, noting her obvious check of the time.

"Neither," Hailey replied, trying to be nice. "I think time would go a lot faster if there were actually kids wanting to see Santa. But the entire store is practically deserted! I didn't understand why we had to start the Santa visits before Thanksgiving anyway. It seems rather pointless to me, but I'm generally opposed to hearing Christmas music right after Halloween too."

"So you're a Scrooge." Santa said, his eyes sparkling with amusement.

"Before Thanksgiving? Definitely, yes. I promise to turn into a merry little elf on Black Friday though."

Santa was quiet, though Hailey felt him studying her out of the corner of his eye. She had to admit, Santa's conversation wasn't pushy or extremely annoying, but by his overly attentive manner, Hailey suspected he was interested in her for more reasons than just to pass a boring shift with a coworker. From watching his body language and the upper part of his face that was visible, he appeared to be a relatively young Santa. And it wasn't as if Hailey already had a boyfriend or even a decent list of prospects. Yet it was difficult to not be put off by the long white beard and plump red suit. If this was God's idea of a Prince Charming for Hailey Rhodes, she really didn't know that she could appreciate His sense of humor.

"How about we make things less boring for you with a friendly little wager?" Santa asked, his eyes flashing a mischievous glint.

"What do you mean?" Hailey asked warily. She was not the gambling sort. But in the last two hours, there had been a total of three children come to visit Santa. Hailey had instead spent the time rearranging every item in the display area and trying to avoid Santa's many attempts to draw her into a conversation. It wasn't that Hailey was unfriendly, but she wasn't a social butterfly. She was already in a bad mood and really couldn't imagine having that much in common with a department store Santa Claus. But at this point, she was getting desperate for almost any distraction. Counting the tiles on the ceiling was beginning to look like a fascinating use of her time. Now if Santa had a better idea…

"I think you're wrong about it being a mistake to start the Santa visits so early. I'm willing to bet you that we will have over a hundred kids come to see us before the end of our shift."

"Are you joking?" Hailey asked. "It's the middle of the day. Nobody is going to be coming to see Santa. Parents are at work, and kids are at school. Our shift ends at 6:00. There's nobody in the store right now. I don't see how that is going to change."

Santa shrugged. "Take it or leave it."

"What are the stakes?" Hailey asked. The man didn't appear insane, but if he was foolish enough to make a silly wager, she might just take him up on it.

"If you win and we have less than 100 kids come, then I will give you a $50 gift card to the store."

"And if you win?" Hailey asked.

"You go on a date with me."

Excerpt: The Romance of the Sugar Plum Fairy

ENJOY this special excerpt from *The Romance of the Sugar Plum Fairy*, available now.

"I'M going to ask you one more time, Calyssa. Please reconsider."

"We've already gone over this before, Peter. It isn't as if you haven't known it was coming."

"We need you." Peter's tone was adamant, making the statement as if everything had already been decided and the case closed.

Peter Remsky was a force. Having been extraordinarily successful as the owner and manager of a highly acclaimed touring ballet company, he was used to getting his own way.

"You have other talented dancers who can fill my place," Calyssa sighed wearily. "And they're much younger than I am. It's time I retired from professional ballet. 'The Nutcracker' will be my last performance."

"The idea of Calyssa Durant retiring is ridiculous!" Peter burst out, throwing his hands up in exasperation. "You haven't been injured. You're still at your peak. Many ballerinas dance past their mid-thirties, and some make it to mid-forty."

"But I'm not them."

"You're right; you're much more talented and skilled than they are," Peter contended. "Being a dancer is who you are."

"And I will still be a dancer. But I want something else out of my life too." Calyssa walked over to the single window in the office. Thoughtfully, she looked out, though the view of the alleyway was anything but inspiring. "I'm thirty-two. I have no family. No hobbies. Dancing has been my entire life since I was eight years old. It's past time that changed."

"Calyssa, I see you when you dance," Peter's tone gentled, his usual boisterous voice and grandiose hand gestures for once calming. "The beauty of your dancing isn't just in your movements; it exudes out of you. You become the dance and the joy you communicate to the audience is something unique. You are the most beautiful dancer I've seen in my life. It's a part of who you are. You can't hide your love for it. How can you even think of quitting?"

"I'm not quitting," Calyssa insisted, trying yet again to reassure her employer. "I'll continue to dance, but in what form, I'm not sure yet. Maybe choreography, maybe a dance school, maybe something else entirely."

Calyssa left the window and returned to Peter, her mind scrambling to find a new way to explain her decision. This was not a new conversation, but no matter what she said, she still had yet to convince Peter that this decision was what was best for her.

"I can't continue on as I have been, Peter," she said finally. "I've been with this troupe—with you—for seven years. We travel constantly. I'm tired. This can't be all there is for me." Calyssa sighed, shutting her eyes briefly. "There's no way to explain except to say that I hear the applause and it no longer thrills me. I don't have a home. My life consists of dancing and sleeping. Nothing else. If I don't quit now, the way I feel is going to start affecting my dancing. I'm not willing to continue while my skill slowly diminishes. I have to retire from my professional career now before I lose what I love."

"It doesn't have to be all or nothing, Calyssa. We can work something out. If you only want to tour for six months, we can deal with that. We'll design a schedule that works for you."

Calyssa looked Peter in the eye, her voice firm, "Saturday will be my last performance."

Calyssa saw the protest on Peter's face even before he opened his mouth. With dread, she realized that no matter what she said, he wouldn't be willing to accept her decision or drop the topic. She mentally braced herself for the grand and persuasive speech she knew Peter was about to deliver.

However, at the unexpected sound of someone clearing his throat, the words on Peter's lips were cut off. Startled, Calyssa quickly turned to find a tall man leaning against the doorframe of the office, as if he'd been there a while.

"I don't mean to interrupt… " the man said, his voice deep.

"Not at all!" Peter quickly bustled forward with his usual nervous energy and an outstretched hand.

As the men shook hands, Calyssa tried to hide her embarrassment and the telltale reddening of her complexion. Exactly how long had this man been standing there? Had he heard everything she'd said—even her age and talk of her hum-drum life?

"So glad you could make it, Nik!" Peter was saying. "And thanks so much for letting us use the facilities for the Christmas party."

"No problem," Nik replied. "You have full use of the facilities and anything else you need while you're here. I'm sorry we couldn't have provided a better office for you. This one is on my list to remodel."

Peter brushed aside his apology with a wave. "Think nothing of it. This will do nicely for the next week. Some theaters we visit don't have an extra office available, so I have to use a corner backstage. By comparison, this room is the Hilton!"

As they spoke, Calyssa unobtrusively inspected the newcomer through lowered lashes. Unfortunately, she realized his appearance only made her discomfort worse. Whoever this "Nik" was, he looked distinguished and breathtakingly handsome with dark, wavy hair, strong features, and warm chocolate-colored eyes.

Calyssa only got the full impact of those eyes when he suddenly looked her direction. She didn't turn away quick enough, and their gazes met as if drawn together by magnets.

Despite his upper-class air, the eyes that met Calyssa's held humor. As his mouth creased up at the corners in a knowing smile, Calyssa looked away in embarrassment. She knew then that he'd heard everything.

Peter was a long-time friend. Calyssa really thought of him as a favorite uncle. She didn't mind discussing her feelings and ambitions with him, but having her personal life laid bare for a stranger was disconcerting.

Seeming to notice the direction of Nik's gaze, Peter turned toward Calyssa as well. "Oh, let me introduce you to one of our performers. Nikolas Clauson, I'd like you to meet Calyssa Durant. Calyssa has been our prima ballerina for years. She's currently playing the role of the Sugar Plum Fairy. Unfortunately, Calyssa's current plan is to leave us at the end of this run. I'm not sure how we're going to manage without her."

Calyssa accepted Nik's firm handshake and tried to hold his sharp gaze steady despite her lingering embarrassment.

"Well, your loss may be my gain," Nik said with interest. Turning his full attention to Calyssa, he explained. "This isn't the first time Peter has mentioned the upcoming change in your career. Though I'm sure he still has plans to attempt to convince you to abandon your plans, I have some opportunities you may be interested in."

"Nik is the owner of this theater," Peter explained. "I've known his family for a long time. Nik has wanted our company to come perform for several years now, but you know how in-demand we are and how far out we book our schedule. Now that we're finally here, he apparently has plans of stealing you to go along with his ambitions for his theater." Peter looked at his watch. "Sorry, Nik, you're going to have to work your charms on Calyssa later. We have a Christmas party to attend."

As Peter led the way out of the office, Nik fell back to walk with Calyssa. "May I take you to dinner, Miss Durant? Maybe you're free after the party?"

As Calyssa looked at him in confusion, Nik rushed to explain, "To discuss the opportunities, of course." Yet his face held an obvious glint of humor, and as Calyssa looked up at him, he gave a slow, deliberate wink.

Calyssa eyed him in amusement.

He was flirting!

"I think I'd like that," she found herself saying, responding automatically. "That is, discussing opportunities, of course."

As they entered the theater lobby, Peter quickly confiscated Nik's attention, ending Calyssa's hope of a continued conversation. Soon, Calyssa lost sight of Nik as Peter paraded him around for introductions with others deemed important.

Though the lobby was large, it was filled with a corresponding large number of people. It was a well-staffed traveling ballet troupe, and anyone who was connected in any way to the production was in attendance at the annual Christmas party.

As Calyssa scanned the ornate room, she felt bittersweet waves of emotion crowding close. The people in this room had been her family for the last seven years. This was her last Christmas party with them. After this week, she would be telling them goodbye and starting a new chapter in her life. And, chances were good that the new chapter would not include many of the friends she'd made here.

Calyssa wanted to enjoy tonight and this last week, but it was difficult to shake her introspective mood. Not feeling yet like participating in any of the boisterous pockets of conversation gathering around the room, Calyssa headed for the food table.

As she chose a few hors d' oeuvres and placed them on a small paper plate, she heard Peter clear his throat from midway up the red-carpeted staircase. As typical, he'd wasted no time.

"Gifts for everyone!" the jolly man shouted as he descended the staircase and began handing out brightly-wrapped packages to each of his employees.

Everyone gleefully joined his playful attitude, pretending to be surprised as they were each called by name to come accept a box. It wasn't as if they didn't already know what it was. Peter Remsky gave the same gifts in the same manner every year, and though calling each recipient by name was a bit drawn out, no one in the ballet troupe would have had it any other way.

Though less enthusiastic than the others, Calyssa accepted her box and Peter's accompanying kiss to the cheek with a smile. This would be the last year she would be here to accept Peter's traditional gift.

Calyssa took the festive gift to one of the less-populated corners of the room and slowly opened it, savoring the experience just a bit. Though she refused to rethink her decision, seven years with the same tradition made for a bittersweet finale.

She untied the festive red ribbon and carefully lifted the gold-wrapped lid. Nestled inside the rather large box was a small paper—a check.

Every year, Peter's traditional Christmas party was always on the first night at their last location before Christmas, typically a Sunday. There he gave his employees a Christmas bonus check, each wrapped in its own large, elaborate box. Everyone would then have the rest of the night and all day Monday to celebrate and waste their money before needing to return for the final run of shows.

The room was loud with laughter as the gifts were opened and met with grandiose expressions of surprise. Calyssa glanced at the amount on her check. It was more than she usually received as a Christmas bonus, and she was reasonably certain Peter had included the extra as a special gift just for her.

Calyssa's thoughts were suddenly interrupted.

"Do you want to come out with the rest of us tonight, Calyssa?" her friend, Felicia, asked as she approached.

Felicia was the "costume mistress" for the ballet troupe, and much to Calyssa's amusement, her friend always looked the part. Felicia liked to use her skills to design and sew her own clothes, though Calyssa thought a more accurate term would be 'costumes.' Tonight's creation was a bit on the gaudy end of the spectrum. As usual, Felicia's dark, curly hair was mounted on her head with a variety of colorful scarves, while her one-shouldered cocktail dress boasted large sections of red and hot pink muddied together. The lime green belt cinching in her waist completed her ensemble.

"No, thanks, Felicia" Calyssa replied, fitting the lid back on the box. "I'm not really in the partying mood." She didn't feel the need to mention that she already had plans with a certain theater owner. "You guys go spend your money and have fun. I'll probably try to get out and do some sightseeing tomorrow."

"By yourself?" Felicia asked, incredulous. "Come on, Calyssa! I know you've never been much for partying, but this is our last stop—your last stop. Besides, you've been moping around and being downright antisocial lately. Are you sure you want to quit?"

"I haven't been moping, Felicia! And, yes, I am very sure. This is my last stop. I've probably been a little quieter lately, but definitely not moping!"

Felicia actually rolled her eyes. "I don't understand why you're quitting. Sure, you're older, but you're still a good dancer. You haven't had an injury. And it's not like you really have any other interests other than dancing. Ballet is the only thing you like to do. You'll probably take and hoard your Christmas bonus and not do anything fun. That's just not normal, Calyssa. I'm going to take and spend my bonus and have a blast doing it.

"Although... " Felicia said, pausing thoughtfully. "If I could get a gift like *him*, I would gladly trade in my check right now."

Calyssa followed Felicia's gaze to see Nik standing with a group about halfway across the room.

When you travel with a group and know everyone, someone new sticks out like a sore thumb. And this was especially true of Nik. With his dark good-looks and distinguished appearance, Calyssa imagined he was undoubtedly under surveillance by nearly every female in the room.

As Calyssa watched, Nik suddenly looked her direction,

as if he felt her eyes on him. Their gazes caught and held. Even from a distance, Calyssa recognized the subtle turning up of the corners of his mouth in another knowing little smile. Calyssa looked away quickly, searching for something—anything—to pretend an absorbing interest in. He knew she'd been watching him.

Felicia, however, had no qualms about continuing to openly stare. She whispered. "I bet *he* could find a way to get you out of your funk. Calyssa, you need a man."

Calyssa opened her mouth to retort but was interrupted before any sound of protest could be made.

"Excuse me, it's Felicia, right?"

Calyssa turned to see a tall, dark-haired woman in a low-cut, fuchsia cocktail dress addressing her friend. Compared to the rather ostentatious attire of these two women, Calyssa was beginning to feel a bit drab in her little black dress.

"Yes," Felicia answered, "and you're Trish, if I remember right." Felicia turned to Calyssa. "Trish works here at the theater. She helped me get everything organized backstage this afternoon. Thanks for your help, by the way," she said, turning back to Trish. "Moving day is always crazy. That's why it's so nice to get everything done and have Monday off."

"No problem," Trish said with a friendly smile. "We're excited to have your troupe here. I know my daughter is really looking forward to seeing 'The Nutcracker.' I've heard wonderful things about it and about your performance especially, Calyssa. I'm happy to meet you, though I think you've already met my husband. At least, I thought I saw you speaking with him earlier."

In confusion, Calyssa looked at Trish then followed the direction of the woman's bright gaze.

Calyssa's heart dropped to the floor.

With her mouth suddenly feeling like cotton, Calyssa forced herself to ask the obvious question. "And your husband is… ?"

"Nik Clauson, of course."

YESTERDAY SERIES

ALL six thrilling tales of time-travel in Amanda Tru's best-selling saga, the *Yesterday Series*, are available now in newly edited editions, complete with discussion questions for individuals or book clubs and all new timeline diagrams.

The Yesterday Series:

Book 1: Yesterday

Book 2: The Locket

Book 3: Today

Book 4: The Choice

Book 5: Tomorrow

Book 6: The Promise

Proudly published by *Sign of the Whale Books™*, a division of *Olivia Kimbrell Press™*.

SNEAK PEEK

ENJOY this sneak peek into **Yesterday**, book 1 in the **Yesterday** series, available now wherever fine books are sold.

RED flashed against the bright white of the snow.

I slammed on the brakes. The SUV skidded toward the guardrail.

My heart seemed to stop. I couldn't breathe. My body felt suspended as the mountainous terrain whirled across my vision. I braced for impact. Unexpectedly, the vehicle lurched as the tires found traction and came to a sudden stop

I sucked in air. My eyes frantically searched the heavy snowfall.

What had I seen?

Was it human?

Had I hit something?

The Sierra mountains were shrouded in the stillness of the winter storm, silent and revealing no secrets. Had I just imagined something dart in front of me?

I caught a glimpse of a fist out of the corner of my eye. I jumped. A strangled scream escaped my throat as the fist started hammering on my window. Heart thumping, I peered beyond the relentless pounding to see the outline of a woman in a red parka. She was screaming, but I couldn't understand her words.

Fingers fumbling and shaking, I rolled down my window. At her appearance, an electric current of shock ripped through me.

Blood streamed from somewhere on her head. It trickled down to her chin, leaving a dark red trail. Dirty tears streaked her cheeks, and her hair hung in clumps of frizzy knots.

I frantically jerked open my door.

"Are you okay?" I asked.

But she didn't answer. Instead, she continued to scream, her hysterical cries now slicing through me.

"Help! Help! Please help me! I can't get them out!"

What was she talking about? My eyes traced an invisible line to where she was gesturing. A few yards in front of my own fender, the meager guardrail was bent and scraped. Peering through the falling snow, I could see beyond that to where the frozen earth had been torn up. Standing on the frame of my car door, I looked into the embankment off the side. Red tail lights glowed like beacons.

The shock to my senses was like a physical blow. I

sprang out of the car, stepping into a blood stained patch of snow. Blood had dripped from the woman's leg where her torn pants exposed a jagged wound. Her sobbing and frantic cries continued, but she wasn't making sense.

Her skin was chalky green. She was in shock, yet I felt paralyzed. My medical background consisted of a three hour CPR and first aid class I'd taken over a year ago. Panic washed over me like a wave. I didn't know how to help her!

Desperate, I gently pushed her toward the back seat of the SUV. Her feet shuffled forward two steps, and then she collapsed. I caught her around the shoulders and practically dragged her rag doll frame to the back seat.

She roused enough to help as I lifted her into the back seat. I unraveled the scarf from my neck and wrapped it around her leg above the bloody gash, tying it as tightly as I could.

Reaching into the back of the SUV, I located a large flashlight and my old coat that I used when skiing. I wrapped the arms of the coat loosely around her leg, hoping the bulky material would soak up some of the blood.

"What's your name?" I asked the woman.

She cleared her throat and shook her head, her brow creasing with confusion. Instead, she began a new litany of faint but frantic cries about her family.

"You can tell me later. I'm Hannah."

"Help! My family… !"

"I'm going down into the ravine right now. Stay here. I'll help them. I promise."

Hoping I didn't just make a promise I couldn't keep, I shut the door and tripped my way through the snowdrifts toward the red haloed taillights.

I pulled my phone out of my coat pocket. There usually wasn't cell phone coverage on this road. But, just maybe…

No service.

This wasn't supposed to be happening! I should be at my sister's lodge at the top of the mountain not crawling down a steep embankment to help accident victims!

It wasn't even supposed to be snowing! I'd checked the weather report at least a dozen times: no new snow for the next week. Now it was practically a blizzard!

I took deep breaths, trying to control the panic and adrenaline running through my veins as I half climbed, half slid down the incline. This wasn't me. I'm not the brave sort. In fact, I'm pretty much a wimp!

I was facing the risk of a serious panic attack even before any of this had happened. The rational part of my brain said my fear was ridiculous. The roads were supposed to be clear. I'd driven to Silver Springs many times before. And, I was driving the biggest, meanest, previously-owned SUV an over-protective father could buy for his college-age daughter. Despite my best rationale, my hands were sweating, my heart was beating erratically, and I was still at the bottom of the mountain.

But those symptoms were nothing compared to what I experienced now. When my eyes collided with the blue sedan at the bottom, I wanted to turn around and run. The front of the car was wrapped around a tree. How could anyone survive an accident like this?

The gas station attendant's ramblings from earlier replayed in my head like a bad movie. Something about a tragic accident on this same road five years ago. The family had all died.

Taking a deep breath, I felt renewed determination run through my veins as it hitched a ride on an abundance of adrenaline. I had to do this.

"Hello, can anyone hear me?" I called as I slid the last few feet to the bottom of the ravine. My wrist scraped over some exposed branches on the way down, but the pain didn't register. I called again, louder.

No answer.

I didn't want to do this! I didn't want to see the scene inside the mangled car. I drew in a shaky, hiccuping breath.

Reaching the driver's side door, I shined the flashlight inside. The beam flickered in my shaking hand. I counted three passengers, motionless and unresponsive to the bright light. My stomach flipped as the beam caught blood marring each pale face.

I bent over, hyperventilating and gasping for breath. I couldn't do this! They were probably already dead! I closed my eyes. "Please, God, I can't do this! Help me!"

I released my breath slowly, then quickly swung my flashlight back inside before I lost my nerve.

About the Author

AMANDA TRU loves to write exciting books with plenty of unexpected twists. She figures she loses so much sleep writing the things, it's only fair she makes readers lose sleep with books they can't put down!

Amanda has always loved reading, and writing books has been a lifelong dream. A vivid imagination helps her write captivating stories in a wide variety of genres. Her current book list includes everything from holiday romances, to action-packed suspense, to a Christian time travel / romance series.

Amanda is a former elementary school teacher who now spends her days being mommy to three little boys and her nights furiously writing. Amanda and her family live in a small Idaho town where the number of cows outnumber the number of people.

Connect with Amanda Tru online: http://amandatru.blogspot.com/

Author site:

http://amandatru.blogspot.com/

Newsletter email sign up:

http://eepurl.com/ZQdw9

Facebook:

https://www.facebook.com/amandatru.author

Twitter:

https://twitter.com/TruAmanda

GooglePlus+:

https://plus.google.com/+AmandaTru

Pinterest:

http://www.pinterest.com/truamanda/

Goodreads:

https://www.goodreads.com/author/show/5374686.Amanda_Tru